DELIVERING DECKER

The Boys of Fury

KELLY COLLINS

BOOK NOOK PRESS

Chapter 1

HANNAH

His angry eyes stare back at me from strangers' faces. The memory of his laughter poisons my silent moments. His threat makes me fear for my life, but I keep reminding myself he can't hurt me anymore. He already took away everything I held dear. My courage. My hope. My ability to trust. All gone, because he didn't like the word no.

I wanted me back. Not the me that fawned over every handsome man who blew through town, but the me that stood my ground. The girl that didn't take shit from anyone. The woman who could enter hell and come out without a bead of sweat on her brow. What happened to her? What happened to me?

The bell above the diner door rang, and I jumped a foot into the air. When would the jitters end? When would I stop looking over my shoulder waiting for *him* to come after me?

Even without looking at the clock, I knew it was thirty minutes before closing, because Ana and Grace were here, dropping their dripping umbrellas by the door. They walked to the center diner booth to take their regular seats by the window. Mona shuffled behind them and slid onto the end of the cracked, red, leather bench. She was a new addition to the Hannah Banning protection squad. I silently laughed. How would an ancient blind woman help me the next time a man took his frustration out on my face?

They were looking out for me, but their concern was a bitter reminder of Cameron Longfellow's fist to my cheek, the tear to my clothes, and the disregard for my right to choose. No hadn't been a word in that man's vocabulary, but I was sure he'd been screaming it when his father sent him to a rehabilitation center in Europe.

I stopped a few booths down and topped off old man Tucker's mug. "Anything else, Bob?"

He smiled wide enough for his dentures to drop. "If I were younger Hannah, I…" I moved on before he could tell me what he would do. There were some things a girl should not have to see even in her imagination.

The pot of decaf coffee swung back and forth in one hand while three mugs hung from the fingers of the other. "Pie today?" I plopped the mugs on the table with a thud and filled them up. I reached into my apron pocket and pulled out a handful of creamers. Ana and Grace liked their coffee white and sweet. Mona took hers black like her lounge chair, or so she once told me. I had no idea what that meant.

It was the same thing each Wednesday. A cup of decaf and a piece of pie. They claimed it was girl time, but I knew it was their mothering instincts kicking in. Especially when it came to Ana. With Wren only a couple months old, her protection radar scanned every-thing around her, and I was a new blip.

I should've hated her for winning Ryker's heart, but I couldn't. In truth, she was perfect for him in a way I would never be. Then there was Grace. I wanted to hate her too because she had Silas. She'd swooped in and stolen one of the few remaining single men in town who was under sixty, but hating Grace was like hating chocolate. How could I hate something so sweet?

"Do you have that strawberry rhubarb pie?" Mona looked at me, but her eyes never focused on me. They always seem to look beyond me or through me.

"Yep, I've got strawberry rhubarb and cherry and apple." With my pad in hand, I leaned against the booth and waited for them to decide.

Grace doctored her coffee with enough cream to support the dairy industry for a week. "I can't decide between apple and cherry," she said.

"Do you remember when I ordered both?" Ana looked at Grace, her shoulders shaking with laughter. "Choose one because combining them isn't a good plan."

Grace shook her head. "Chapple pie doesn't sound good. Only a pregnant woman would mix the two together." She glanced up at me. "I'll take the cherry."

"I'll take the same," Ana said. She looked around the almost empty diner. "Grab yourself a piece too and come sit with us."

Minutes later, I balanced four plates of pie on one arm and the pot of decaf and a single mug in my other hand. Grace moved next to the window and made room for me.

"Why did Tim put you on the night shift?" she asked.

I forked a piece of apple pie. "Low seniority. I take what shifts he gives me." I didn't have much choice. I needed money. Although the night shift wasn't ideal for a woman who jumped at her shadow, I couldn't turn it down. Too many people depended on me. I wouldn't let them down.

Bob rose from his seat and tossed a bill on the table. "See you soon, Hannah." That meant he'd be back when his Social Security check came in.

"Looks like Bob is sweet on you," Grace said. "I'm so glad he moved on from me. The man was always at my door with one thing or another, but he is a sweetheart."

"He's always been a good man. Those are hard to find these days." Mona wiped the red glaze from her lips and tossed her napkin to the table. "His wife was my best friend for years. We used to go see Thunder Down Under in Denver every year they came to town." Her silver-blue eyes crinkled in the corners when she smiled. "Bob would hand Avis a pile of dollar bills. He told her to enjoy herself, but to bring her appetite home. I'm not sure who loved that one day a year more, Bob or Avis. Older men usually get a six-pack of beer and a lay on their birthdays. Bob got it on his birthday *and* when the strippers came to town."

"Not a vision I want in my head, Mona." I pushed my half-eaten piece of pie away and rose from the seat. "Speaking of dollars." I walked to where Bob had sat, picked up the dollar bill he'd left, and shoved it into my pocket. "I better go and earn mine." I cleared the table and walked toward the counter.

The owl clock above the kitchen window ticked loudly. Its eyes moved from side to side, keeping time with the seconds. The double doors to the kitchen flew open, making my heart thump hard in my chest. I didn't need to wait for Cameron to come after me. I'd die of heart failure long before then.

"I'm outta here, Hannah." The cook pulled his sweat-stained bandana from his head and walked out the front door into the rain.

"What an asshole," Grace said loud enough for her voice to echo through the empty diner. "He should stay and help you lock up. We wouldn't be so worried if there was someone closing the place with you." She stabbed the last bite of her pie and shoved it into her mouth.

Once I added up their tab, I walked back and slid the bill across the table. "I don't need you here. I'm fine."

"I'm blind, sweetheart, and I can see you jump each time something startles you."

I rolled my eyes, knowing only Ana and Grace would see. "I'm fine. I don't need a damn babysitter." With their empty plates gathered in my hands, I turned and walked away.

"You need to see a therapist," Ana blurted out. "You can't get assaulted like you did and not have some lasting effects."

I looked around the diner. "The last time I looked at my benefits package, it didn't come with a mental health plan. I'm lucky to get a free meal."

"You need to talk to someone. You're wound up as tight as a trick yo-yo." Grace drained her coffee mug and slapped it back on the table. The loud noise sent my pulse racing.

"I talk to myself when I'm alone." I swiped up the cups. The owl clock hooted nine times behind me. "We're closed." I appreciated their concern, but there was nothing they could do to help me.

Mona stood and stepped in front of me. "I'm not a therapist, but I want you to come by my house tomorrow. I've found that sometimes chatting can be therapeutic. Besides, I make the best lemonade in the county."

Ana and Grace nodded in agreement.

"That's a great idea. Mona is a great sounding board. Cheapest therapy I ever received," Grace said.

Mona laughed as she walked toward the door. "I told you I was cheap, but I'm not easy." She turned and stared right through me like she saw into my wounded soul. "You better show up, or I'll have to send Marty looking for you, and he hates missing his daytime soaps."

We walked to the door. As soon as they were gone, I locked the place down like it was Fort Knox. The girls were right. I was scared to death to close the diner. On several occasions, I'd considered sleeping in Tim's cot in the back room so I didn't have to walk into a dark desolate parking lot. God only knew what was hiding behind the dumpster or the building. If I could be attacked in broad daylight, there was no telling what could happen under the shadow of night.

I married the ketchup bottles and filled the sugar containers all the while humming some senseless tune. It helped to have background noise because it filtered out the nightmare that lived in the recesses of my mind.

Get on your knees, he'd yelled that day. His fingers had tugged at my braid until I'd been forced to collapse in front of him—in front of the bulge in his pants. *You don't walk away from me.* The memory of his voice ran through my head like chainsaw. It buzzed incessantly at my self-preservation. It chipped at my self-esteem. *You're going to like it, Hannah. You might scream the first time, but then you'll beg for it.*

"*I hate you!*" I screamed. The sugar jar left my hand at a velocity I had no idea I was capable of and hit the wall with such force that it shattered into tiny shards. "Screw you, Cameron Longfellow. You are not allowed in my head anymore."

I pulled out my phone and dialed my sister because somehow her silly self made everything seem all right.

"What's up, sis?" Stacey answered with a smile attached to her voice.

"Hey, Stace, how's it going?" Already my heart rate had slowed and calmed. She had a way of putting things into perspective. She was the reason I worked this shift. She made everything worth the fear I endured. "How's school?" I missed the days when we met at the student union for coffee and bitched about our professors.

She was a year behind me. My little sister had followed me to UC Boulder for college. She'd taken up education, while I'd studied humanities. I never pictured my sister as a teacher, but then again I'd never imagined my mother to be an addict or my life's ambition to be a waitress.

"It's good. I'm gearing up for finals. I should have never taken a full load this year." Her voice held no sign of stress. Stacey didn't have to worry. That was my job as the big sister. Besides, it wasn't part of her makeup. Stacey did what she wanted and worried about the consequences later. Long ago, we both had done that, but that was before my life turned to shit. Cameron Longfellow wasn't the beginning of my downward spiral. He was the end of my long fall into misery.

I slapped on a smile, hoping it would influence the tone of my voice. "You've got this."

Being her cheerleader was the best part of being the big sister. To focus on her meant I didn't have time to focus on me; whether it was a blessing or curse, I wasn't sure yet. But I knew the minute she walked across the stage and snagged her diploma, it would be worth it. One of us deserved a good life.

"Maybe." There was a moment of silence, which was unusual for Stacey because most days she was like a hyperactive kid who devoured the entire inventory of a candy store. When she stopped to contemplate was the time I started to worry.

"What aren't you telling me?"

"Nothing. Everything is great. More than great." Her voice hit that pitch that it achieved only when she was being dishonest.

"Stace?" I kicked at the pieces of broken glass spread across the floor. "Spill it."

There was a moment of silence. "You won't believe who showed up last night." The pitch of her voice hit a nervous high C. "Mark is in town." It was so quiet I could hear the crickets beyond the closed front door chirp into the night.

"No, Stacey. You need to stay away from him. He's trouble."

"Don't worry about me. I've got this under control. He and I were always good together."

"Stace, he's bad news. Let him go," I pleaded.

It was no use. Mark was probably already shacked up in her dorm room, and she was going to get drowned in his tsunami of bullshit. The man was a menace. He had been trouble since the first day he started seeing my sister. She was seventeen when he pulled up on a motorcycle and told her to get on. That started a tumultuous relationship between the three of us. I loved Stacey, but I hated Mark Van Hauser. The day he left Stacey with a broken heart was the worst day of her life, but the best day of mine. That was nearly two years ago, and now he was back. That couldn't be good.

"I gotta go, sis. Mark is waiting downstairs."

"Stacey, don't do—" The phone went dead before I could finish my sentence. I pocketed it and went back to cleaning up my mess. Something told me I'd be cleaning up another one of Stacey's before too long. The universe wouldn't give me a damn break.

A loud bang came from the front door, and I ducked behind the counter. Peeking around the corner, I saw a man leaning on the diner door. His clothes were sopping wet. His right hand cradled his bloody left arm.

Chapter 2

DECKER

I picked the gravel out of my bleeding arm, then pressed my face to the window of the diner. It was the only place that was open. I knew this because I'd limped all the way from one side of town to the other.

My only alternative was to stop at the sheriff's station, which I assumed was manned all the time, but the last thing I needed was trouble. It was bad enough I was where I wasn't supposed to be. On top of that, I'd been on the back of a rented Harley. My parents would never understand.

Inside the diner, which was straight out of a '50s sitcom, was a woman who dashed behind the counter the minute she saw me.

Blood dripped from my fingertips to the wet concrete walk where it mixed with the puddled water and disappeared.

Fisted up, I pounded on the front door. "I know you're in there. Let me in." Endless minutes passed by with no response. "I'm hurt, and I need to make a phone call." I reached into my cargo pants for my phone and pressed the spider-webbed screen to the glass. "See, my phone is broken."

A mass of blonde hair peeked around the corner of the counter for a second time. "Go away."

Although the voice was strong, there was a tinge of fear to it like she thought I was there to hurt her. If she'd only come to the door, she'd see I was in no condition to hurt anyone. I was the one hurt. One glance at my asphalt-skinned arm made it burn even more. Why was that?

"Come on. I'm hurt, I'm bleeding, and I need some help."

"I'll call the police!" she yelled.

Forehead pressed to the cold glass door, I pleaded, "Please don't. I crashed my motorcycle into a tree down the road. I need to wash this wound and call for a ride. That's all. I need your help."

She tiptoed toward the door. When the lock turned, I stumbled back. Standing on the other side of the glass door was a beautiful blonde. In one hand, she held a phone; in the other, a knife. Not even a sharp knife, but a butter knife.

I pushed past the door and stood on the black and white checked floor dripping blood and water all over the entry. Her nametag mocked me with its smiley face stickers surrounding her name. "Hannah. If you're going to stab me, do it now, and put me out of my misery."

Her eyes widened and her shoulders stiffened at the mention of her name. She brandished the dull knife in front of her like a sword. "This is for my protection." She waved it around like a magic wand. The only thing missing was a spell.

"What are you going to do with a butter knife? Death by jelly?" I dropped my chin and saw the blood pooling on the floor beside me. "I'm more likely to bleed out waiting for you to help me than succumb to a death by buttering."

"How do you know my name?" Her voice hovered above a whisper.

I nodded toward her chest.

"Right." Her fingers brushed over the raised letters on her nametag. "What happened to you?" She inched her way to the counter, never turning her back to me.

"Crashed a motorcycle into the tree. You've got some shitty roads in this town." Once we got to the counter, I slid onto the round seat at the end. "Hit a puddle of water, and that's all she wrote."

Hannah reached under the counter. At this point, I wasn't sure what she'd bring out next. Butcher knife? Rolling pin? Cheese grater? She plopped a first-aid kit on the counter, and I relaxed.

"Decided I'm not here to rape you and pillage the place?" Her face turned white when I mentioned rape. My stomach clenched. I reached out to touch her hand, to let her know that my intentions were good, but she pulled back. "I'm not going to hurt you, sweetheart. Do I look like the dangerous type?"

She stared at me for a long minute. "You'd be surprised what dangerous looks like these days."

I reached into my back pocket and pulled out my wallet. "My name is Dex Riley. My father is Rip Riley." I watched her face for recognition, but there wasn't any. The woman had to live under a rock to not know my family name. Riley Realty was the third-largest land brokerage firm in the country. We did everything from property sales to community development.

"You're not from here." She pulled a dry towel from a cabinet and held it under running water at a nearby sink.

"No, I'm from Golden." That was usually home, but the past few nights I'd been staying at a hotel in Boulder, visiting with my dad during the day and trying to clear my head at night.

She pressed the terry cloth against my skin.

An uncontrolled hiss pressed through my lips. "Shit, that hurts."

She dabbed at the wound, trying to get the tiny bits of dirt and rock loose. "If you think it hurts now … wait until tomorrow." Her soft fingers probed around the worst part of the wound. "You could use a few stitches."

"I'm not going to the doctor," I snapped.

"Don't kill the messenger." She opened the cap to some kind of clear ointment that, when applied, soothed the hot fire burning below the surface of my torn-up skin. "I'm giving you my professional opinion."

"You run a clinic in the back next to the ovens?" I wasn't trying to be an asshole, but my whole body ached. Worse than that, my pride ached.

With a yank, she pulled my arm toward her and began wrapping my wound from elbow to wrist in white gauze. "I wasn't always a waitress."

"So it would seem." I looked at her handiwork and nodded. She'd wrapped my injury like a professional—tight and tidy. "Thanks for fixing me up." I looked past her to the counter where three pies sat. I hadn't eaten for hours. "I'll take a piece of cherry pie," I said.

She slammed the first-aid kit shut. "We're closed."

My head fell back, and I groaned. "Really?" I pushed myself to my feet and walked behind the counter. With the knife she'd threatened me with earlier, I cut two pieces of pie and slid them onto clean plates that sat nearby. "Have some pie with me, Hannah. Let me use your phone, and then I'll be on my way." I patted the stool next to me, and to my surprise, she sat down.

"Most guys I know who ride motorcycles don't ride them in the rain." She forked a piece of pie and pressed it between her lips. Lips that were naturally full and lush.

"I could tell you I'm not like most guys, but that would probably be a lie. The truth is, I'm not that experienced with motorcycles." I reached for the half-empty coffeepot she'd left on the counter. She reached for two cups, and I poured us some lukewarm coffee. "It wasn't raining when I left Boulder."

She narrowed her eyes at me. "You said you were from Golden."

I pressed my index finger to the knife I'd used to cut the pie and slid it across the counter to her. "For your protection." I smiled my most charming smile, but she continued to give me an untrusting glare. "I had business in Boulder." The truth was my dad was in the hospital for chemotherapy. "I got restless and rented the damn bike. Drove up here because I might be doing some business in Fury. Wanted to see what it was like."

She played with her pie. "What business would you have in the booming metropolis of Fury?"

"Two brothers contacted my family's firm and asked about finding a broker to start the redevelopment of a neighborhood here."

She sat up straight. "The only brothers I know in Fury are Ryker and Silas."

"Yeah, I think that's them. You know them?"

"Yes, they're good guys." She lifted from her seat and cleared off the dishes in front of us. I waited for her to point me to the door and tell me to leave, but she didn't. "Did you say you needed a phone?" Out of her pocket, she pulled an old flip phone and handed it to me.

"Very retro," I commented.

"Very inexpensive," she tossed back. I liked this girl. She was cautious but friendly. She was scared, and yet she offered me help. Yes, I could already tell that Hannah was a genuinely good person. I didn't meet a lot of them in my circle.

I texted my father's driver and told him where to find me. I called my broken phone from Hannah's so I'd have her number when it was replaced. Then I handed her back her old-school phone.

My wet clothes stuck to my pruned skin, but at least I was warm. Worst case was Hannah would boot me from the diner, and I'd have an hour or so to wait for John to arrive.

"Where's the mop?" I asked.

She tilted her head. "What? Why?"

I looked behind me at the trail of water and blood I'd left in my wake. "I'm not going to leave you with a mess."

"You're in no shape to mop a floor."

I stared down at my bandaged arm. "I'm in better shape now than I was twenty minutes ago. The least I can do is clean up after myself."

She shrugged and walked away. Minutes later a steaming mop bucket pushed through the swinging doors that led from the kitchen.

"You mop, and I'll make fresh coffee. Do you want decaf or regular?"

Something told me I wasn't going to get much sleep as it was. "Fully loaded, please."

Fifteen minutes later, the floors were cleaned, and Hannah's side work, as she called it, was completed. We sat in a booth in the front of the restaurant, sipped coffee, and talked.

"If you weren't always a waitress, what were you?"

She leaned back and stretched her legs out on the booth bench across from me. "I was studying to be a social worker, but you know… life happens."

"Social workers have to learn first aid?"

She laughed, and it was a beautiful sound. Light and airy and sweet like pink cotton candy. "No, my mom *was* a nurse, and I learned first aid from her."

She put emphasis on the word *was*, which intrigued me. "Is she still working? At what hospital?" Maybe she was at Boulder General and I'd run into her while visiting Dad.

Hannah's shoulders slumped. It looked like her life wasn't all smiley faces after all.

"It's a long story. Maybe another day." She sipped her coffee and stared blankly across the diner. "What about your family?"

I looked out the window. The rain had stopped, and only a light mist came down. "Another long story better saved for another day."

In the distance, headlights broke through the haze. As they neared, I recognized the black town car as John's.

"Your ride?"

"Yep." I laid a twenty on the table and scooted out of the booth. "Hannah, thank you so much for being such a nice person."

"It was nice to meet you, Dex." She followed me to the door. "Take care of your arm."

"Will do." Something made me want to bend over and kiss her cheek or pull her in for a hug. Something made me want to wrap this girl up in my arms and take her home, but all I did was turn toward her and smile. "Are you going to be okay closing up by yourself? I could wait for you."

She unlocked the door and stepped aside so I could exit. "I'll be fine." She looked over her shoulder toward the kitchen. "I've got a butter knife."

Chapter 3

HANNAH

I looked left and right, scouring the dark for Cameron. It was a hard habit to break.

I felt around the inside of my purse for the house key. Despite the glow of the television showing through the lace curtains, no one would come to my aid if I screamed. Mom would be too out of it to get up and investigate.

The news played loudly in the background, muffling the creak of the rusty hinges. I rushed inside and locked the door behind me. The best part of my day was when I was safe in the house.

Sprawled out on the worn sofa was Mom. At least this time a bottle didn't hang from her fingers, and her clothes appeared clean. On the flip side, her pain-pill bottle lay on its side, empty.

It pissed her off that I hid her prescription and left only two pills a day, but in some sick way, I was proud that she was down to two. A year ago she was hustling anyone she could to get her fix. She teetered between booze and drugs, depending on which was easier to get. It was sad to see how far she'd fallen.

I pulled the pink and green crocheted blanket over her thin shoulders and tucked it under her chin. Once I shut the television off, I schlepped toward my room. My ass dragged like a lead weight behind me. It had been a long day. In fact, all the days seemed to blur together. The wheel of life kept rotating, and I continued to run fast enough to keep up but never get ahead.

A firm toss landed my purse in the corner. I set my phone on the nightstand and plopped onto my bed. The same bed I'd had in high school. The same bed Mom's asshole boyfriend had climbed into and changed everything.

All it took was a blood-curdling scream. The minute that man touched me, Mom ran to me with a loaded gun. She aimed and pulled the trigger. One scream, one bullet, three lives ruined.

My shoes clunked to the floor when I toed them loose. I curled into a ball on top of the pink comforter. Things could have been worse, I supposed. We had survived. At least we were all alive, including the asshole, but that event had started a downward spiral that seemed to be an endless funnel that sucked in the Banning women. Bad men. Bad choices. Bad luck.

I rolled off the bed, onto my sore feet, and readied myself for sleep. But when I climbed under the covers and closed my eyes, I didn't see Mom's asshole boyfriend or Cameron Longfellow lurking in the shadows of my almost dreams. Staring back at me were the bottomless blue eyes of Dex Riley, and for the first time in a long time, I felt better because I'd helped someone who appreciated it. I'd reached past my comfort zone, allowed myself to be vulnerable, and survived. Helping people had always been my goal, and tonight I'd reclaimed a piece of myself.

MOM WAS in the kitchen fussing with the coffeepot when I walked in. She pounded on the start button and waited. Nothing. "Damnit." She opened the lid and glanced inside the water reservoir, then slammed it shut. "If I can't have a damn drink, I need a cup of coffee."

"You need help?" I pushed off the doorjamb and approached her. It wasn't often Mom had the energy to do much. Today was a major event.

I lifted the unplugged cord so she could see why the coffeepot wasn't working. "Electricity helps." I shoved the three-pronged plug into the wall and pressed the power button. "How ya feelin' this morning?" I'd been slowly weaning her off opioids for over a year, and of the two pills a day I left her, one of them was an over-the-counter painkiller that looked remarkably similar to the Oxy she managed to get. Little by little, she was coming back to me. Too bad the first thing to arrive was her temper.

"I feel like shit," she grumbled.

"Good, at least you feel something." I reached past her and pulled the tea bags from the cupboard. The selection was slim because the budget didn't allow for much more than Lipton, but I'd snagged a mint tea packet from the diner in case I ever had something to cele-brate. It was my version of champagne, and the fact that Mom was up and about was a good enough reason to drink it.

"I'll tell you what I feel, young lady." She leaned on the counter and pressed her palm to her head. "I feel like my skull is going to explode from lack of stimulants and my stomach might collapse from lack of food."

"I can fix both." Inside the refrigerator was a tray of cinnamon rolls. Tim always let me bring the day-olds home. These were three-day-old pastries, but a dab of butter and twenty seconds in the microwave would bring them back to life.

"That's what you're good at. You're a fixer."

I rolled my eyes, which years ago would have gotten me a slap up the side of the head; now, Mom hardly cared. "I'm a real success, Mom. I can heat up a donated roll and plug in a pot of coffee."

Mom's expression wasn't as vacant as usual. Even the blue of her irises was brighter. "I'm not talking about coffee and buns, Hannah." She dumped several tablespoons of sugar into the bottom of her cup and waited for the last of the water to sputter into the pot. "I'm talking about how you try to fix everything and everyone." She cupped my cheek. The heat of her palm had me leaning into her touch. I never knew when Mom would go off the rails again, so I had to take her love when I could get it.

"I refuse to give up on you, Mom." I reached under the sink and pressed my hand into the hole in the wall. She often hid alcohol next to the plumbing.

"There's nothing there." Her voice was clipped.

"Good. We're making progress." She didn't like me searching, but I had to. It was a matter of survival—hers. I'd managed to find her hiding spots so far. In our two-bedroom shithole, there weren't many places she could hide stuff, but addicts were clever. I'd found bottles inside the toilet tank. Pills buried in the pots of dead plants. Once I'd found a bag of fermented fruit shoved in a boot in her closet.

Right now she was sober and lucid, but I'd learned to question the quiet before the storm.

"How's work?" Mom poured her coffee while I dunked a tea bag in hot water. I could get two cups of it before it was tasteless.

"It's okay." With a plate of gooey cinnamon rolls and my cup of tea, I led her to the scarred wooden table in the corner. "Some guy showed up last night after he crashed his bike into a tree." I kept my voice even, denying the tension the incident caused. Mom didn't know about the beating I'd taken from Cameron Longfellow. She didn't know about his group of victims showing up to the courthouse. She didn't know about my nightmares. For all intents and purposes, Mom was clueless.

"Those damn motorcycle gangs. Always trouble." It was a risky subject because Mom's old boyfriend Allen Hatch was a biker. Not any biker, but the leader of a gang. When Mom shot him, no one paid attention to my claim that he'd sexually assaulted me. Nope, everyone was afraid of him, even the judge. When I testified, no one believed me. The truth was, they were too afraid not to believe him.

Mom got charged with a firearms violation and endangering a minor. Stacey and I went into the system until I turned eighteen. I went straight to college while my mom went straight to a personal hell. A good beating in the women's correctional facility started her addiction. Her pain at failing her girls and losing her job as an RN ate at her until she drank it away. Then came the stroke, which left her with a literal weak side.

"He's not a gangbanger, Mom. In fact, he rented a motorcycle and didn't have much experience riding one, especially in the rain."

"Not too bright, that one. I hope you're not planning on trying to save him too."

I placed a fork into Mom's hand and pressed the tray of rolls toward her. "I don't have time to save him when all my time is spent trying to save you." It wasn't the nicest thing to say, but I was reaching the end of my patience. We'd get to this point where I was sure she'd turn the corner, and then she'd revert back to the pill-popping alcoholic she'd become over the past several years.

"I'm a shit mother." She dropped her fork and lowered her head.

"Yes, Mom. You are now, but you didn't use to be, and you don't have to be one anymore. You could be that mother who bakes cookies and asks me about my day. You could come to the diner and join me for coffee or tea. You could take a quick trip to Boulder and visit Stacey."

She shook her head. "You don't know what it's like to be scared. You're strong and independent. I'm broken."

You're wrong. Broken and scared were two conditions I knew well. Add lonely, despairing, and abandoned, and I had a royal flush in the card game of life. I didn't have someone to put back the pieces for me like I tried to do for her. Moms were supposed to be there for their kids, and mine was simply absent.

My buried resentment caused me to snap at her. "You're not broken, you're complacent. Get up and fight. If you can't fight for yourself, then fight for Stacey and me. We still need you."

Mom's face turned a shameful red, her failure once again shining for all to see like a neon light. "I'm trying." She drank the last of her coffee and left the empty mug on the table. Walking away, she said, "I'm going back to bed."

Figures. If she couldn't numb her pain, she'd sleep it away.

"I'm heading out to see a friend," I called bitterly to her retreating back. It was funny how moments ago, she sat at the kitchen table across from me, and yet I had to seek out someone else for motherly advice.

"I KNEW you couldn't resist my lemonade." Mona lifted her dark glass and shaded her eyes with her hand. Last night's storm had blown over and left us with a lovely late spring day.

"How did you know it was me?" Mona patted the wicker seat next to her. I sank into the floral cushion that had seen better days. There were several empty glasses sitting on the table. I wasn't sure whether Mona kept them at the ready in case someone showed up, or in the hopes that someone would.

She picked up the pitcher and filled a glass while she spoke. "I see in shadows, and what I've lost in my eyesight, I've picked up in other senses. You couldn't be Ana or Grace because they both carry babies, which makes their silhouette larger. Besides, they smell like baby powder or baby poop—both scents stick in your nose hairs like glue. Ryker and Silas are built like oak trees, so they cast a shadow on the porch long before they reach it. Marty uses a cane, so he has this distinctive clip-clop that follows him up the walkway. And now that he's getting a little bump and tickle, he whistles a lot."

I took a sip of the tart drink, squinted my eyes, and let the shiver run down my body. I wasn't sure whether it was from the thought of Marty and Mona doing it, or from the tartness of the lemonade. One thing was certain, though, those two doing the deed was not what I wanted to see when I closed my eyes. I didn't need that image adhering to my brain cells.

Better to focus on more pleasant things. "The lemonade is great." She was right; it was the best I'd had in a long time.

"I know," she said. Anyone else saying something like that would have come off as cocky and arrogant, but it was Mona, and she had a way about her that allowed her to say about anything and get away with it.

"How's your mom?"

I shrugged. "It's a good day." At least it had started out a good day. It was still early, and things could change.

"That's good. One day at a time, they say." She looked out over her yard. At least a dozen plastic pink flamingos dotted her grass.

"You like the pink birds?"

She leaned forward toward the yard. "How many are there now? I swear the damn things are breeding."

I counted fourteen in a quick scan of the yard. "They're definitely breeding. You've got more than a dozen. Soon people will describe you as the crazy bird lady."

Mona chuckled. "I've been called worse." She rose from her seat and walked down the sidewalk. She stopped at the edge of her yard like she was counting for herself. "I got one as a joke at a Bunco game thirty years ago, and since then they've kept showing up."

"It could be worse. Someone keeps dumping trash in my neighbor's yard. It was run-down before, but now it looks like the city junkyard."

She grabbed the handrail and dragged herself up the steps and back to her seat. "We need someone to come in here and clean up this town." She looked far away like she was dreaming of another time. "You weren't here back then. But this neighborhood was full of families. The grass was cut, and the flowerbeds were full. I kept a pitcher of lemonade on the table there for anyone who wanted a glass."

"I've heard the stories." Horror stories, to be specific. Now that I'd made friends with Ana and Grace, I knew exactly what this town had gone through before Mom, Stacey, and I showed up. We weren't natives, we were transplants, drawn to Fury years ago because it was cheap to live here and an easy commute for my mom to get to her job at Boulder General Hospital. "Last night this guy came into the diner and said something about brokering a deal between the Savages and a development company."

"They were talking about trying to get someone to come in and breathe life into the neighborhood."

I looked around at all the abandoned houses. "We need more than a breath. We need full-on cardiac support and maybe intubation to survive."

"I thought you were studying to do social work."

"I was, but since I left school, I've been digging into Mom's nursing books. If I ever get the chance to go back, I think I might look into becoming a nurse." I thought about the satisfaction I felt of cleaning up Dex's wound. "Mom says I'm good at fixing things."

"Have you ever been on a plane?" Her question came from Pluto.

"Yes. Once. Mom took us to Disneyland. Why?"

"I was thinking about you and your family, and how you've given up everything to make sure they're okay, but who's there to make sure you're okay?"

The old woman in pin curls and smudged orange lipstick was making no sense. "What does that have to do with flying?"

"At the beginning of the flight, the attendant gets up and demonstrates how to use the safety equipment. At one point, the mask drops down, and they say to put your mask on first and then take care of the child beside you." Mona turned to me and grasped my hand. "Hannah, your mom is the child right now. Isn't it time you put your mask on first?"

Chapter 4

DECKER

O f course, Dad would be in the boardroom when I arrived. He looked at his watch. A pricey Patek Philippe that cost more than the median income of an average Colorado resident.

He leaned over and whispered, "You're late."

I didn't have a forty-thousand-dollar watch to keep me on time. I had a new smartphone, and its digital display proved I was early, but not early enough for Dad.

Leave it to the man to finish chemo and rush right over because he didn't trust that I could hold this meeting without him. I was twenty minutes early and still in trouble because our clients had arrived before me.

I buttoned my jacket and straightened my tie. "Good morning." I walked with false confidence to the large wooden table where the Savage brothers sat, and I shook their hands. Thank God I shook right-handed because I could hardly lift my left arm. "I'm Decker, but everyone calls me Dex."

Both brothers smiled like I'd told them they'd won the lottery. *Weird, but whatever.*

"I'm Ryker," the larger man said before turning to the other man. "This is my younger brother, Silas."

"Nice to meet you. Can I get you coffee or a soda?" I gave Dad a look that said, *you failed to make our clients comfortable.*

"No thanks," Ryker said. Silas shook his head as well.

"Shall we get started?" I grabbed a notepad and pen and sat across from the men. Dad took the seat at the head of the table. Despite his pale complexion and his withering physique, he still had that alpha air about him. That better-than-everyone attitude that always made me uncomfortable. Like somehow, no matter how hard I tried, it would never be enough. Did his take-no-prisoners arrogance make clients uncomfortable too? I'd bet my life on it.

Ryker and Silas seemed unfazed, but then again, making the Savages comfortable wasn't high on Dad's priority list. In fact, this meeting was a waste of time, according to him, because the brothers didn't have any money. Dad allowed the meeting because he thought it would be good practice and low risk. The only thing we lost was time, and mine had no value.

The Savages were interested in finding someone to develop their neighborhood—a neighborhood that died decades ago with several dozen townsfolk. I took the meeting because I'd done some research. Fury's history was a tragedy that could be turned around. With the right investors, the town could thrive. It was a perfect bedroom community for the ever-growing town of Boulder, which meant it had untapped potential. Even though Dad didn't see it that way, deep inside I knew it to be the truth.

One extended breath filled my lungs, and I was as ready as I could be. I was raised with a take-no-prisoners attitude, but inside I was a prisoner. Real estate was my cell; my father, the warden.

We discussed the population, the amenities, the taxes, and the abandoned properties. I didn't confess to driving through Fury yesterday. I didn't want Dad knowing I'd rented a Harley. He was dead set against bikes. His belief was that anyone riding motorcycles lacked sophistication and brains.

Dad rose from the leather throne at the head of the table and walked out with a nod to Ryker and Silas. "My office when you're finished." His clipped and tight voice confused me. Short of not being an hour early, everything had gone well. I asked the right questions. I got the answers I needed to move forward.

Once the brothers were gone, I approached Dad's office with trepidation.

I barely had one wingtip shoe in the door when he started in on me.

"Where the hell were you last night?" He slammed his coffee on the desk, the liquid spilling over the edge. "I left several messages that went unanswered."

I lifted my new phone. "My old one shattered, and I couldn't retrieve messages."

Dad pushed back from his desk and stood. Despite his sickly appearance, he was still intimidating. He never hit me with his hands, only his words.

"You think you can come in here, wearing yesterday's suit and looking like you haven't slept at all, and run a company?"

I pulled on my jacket. It was the same suit I'd worn yesterday, but there wasn't a thing wrong with it. My shirt was freshly pressed and my tie perfectly matched. Feeling tight in the throat, I tugged at the knot so I could speak my mind.

"Seems like I did just that. There isn't a thing wrong with what I'm wearing." It was rare that I mouthed off at Dad, but time for us was running out. Opportunities to voice my opinion were scarce.

"Don't play with me, son. Are you using again?" He stepped into my space, breathed in my air. "My life's investment rests with you, and I'll be damned if I'm going to leave it in the hands of a spoiled boy with substance-abuse problems."

Rage boiled under my skin. "Then keep it," I said. "Keep the whole damn thing." Out the door, I walked.

It had been years since I'd had even an aspirin. One bad year in college, and I was labeled as a habitual offender in Dad's eyes. Cocaine and vodka had been my drugs of choice, but one stint in rehab and a twelve-step program had straightened me out.

It pissed me off that he threw my past in my face and never acknowledged his. The man was dying from pancreatic and liver cancer because twelve steps weren't enough for him.

I marched across the street to Dudley's Diner. Whereas a few years ago I might have run straight for a martini, these days I settled for coffee and pie.

At the counter, I pondered my life. At twenty-three, I'd done everything my parents had asked of me. I had a degree. I passed my realtor licensing exams. I was studying to get my broker's license. What my life felt like most was a lie. These weren't my dreams but Dad's. Everything he built would be mine, and the funny thing was that it didn't feel right. I didn't want it.

I wasn't cut out to wear suits and broker land deals. I ripped at the knot at my neck until the noose was loose and I could breathe again.

"You're becoming a regular, sweetheart." The redheaded waitress leaned on the table with her pad in her hand. "Coffee and pie?"

"Sounds good."

She stared past me to beyond the window. "You're out of place here. Most suits like you dine at Trivoli's across the street."

Yep, my Brooks Brothers ensemble was a stark contrast with the average diner patron's jeans and T-shirt. This wasn't a new problem for me; I'd always felt out of place like I was in the wrong skin or something. "Nope, I'm an apple pie and coffee kind of guy."

"Make yourself at home then." She scribbled my order and disappeared around the counter.

A piece of me hated myself for being such a big disappointment to my dad, but his condition had taught me a valuable lesson. Life was short and uncertain. Dad loved his business more than his family. He thrived on the deal, but each day I pulled on my trousers, buttoned up the crisp shirt, and folded myself into a jacket was another day where I died to get out and be free.

"Here you go, doll." She pushed the pie and coffee in front of me and went on to the next table.

I settled into my seat. For whatever reason, I felt comfortable on a stool at the counter, which I gathered wasn't a common reaction. The only thing that could make it better would be a blonde wielding a butter knife. I liked her. I liked Fury.

I picked up my phone and dialed John. "That girl at the diner last night. I need information. You know what to do." John was more than a driver. He was a friend. He was also the go-to man when anyone needed the 411 on anything, and I wanted to know more about Hannah.

Chapter 5

HANNAH

Tall, dark, and handsome was definitely my type, but once you got past those three attributes of his, Dex failed to resemble anything I'd dated. I'd glommed onto arrogant assholes my whole life, but the man I bandaged up last night wasn't an asshole. He was nice. Definitely not my norm, but wasn't it time for a change? I'd been a jerk magnet long enough. Too bad I'd never see him again.

I walked into the diner and went straight to work. On Thursdays, I had the short afternoon shift, and it was all about cleaning, which meant I'd spend more time on my knees than my feet. Usually, I considered that the worst shift, but today it didn't bother me much.

I shined the stainless steel bases of the stools and smiled when I got to the end. It was the stool Dex had sat at when I bandaged his arm. When I got to the leather benches of the front booths, I didn't even mind digging stray fries out of the crevices because this was the booth where we'd drunk coffee and talked like normal people.

The bell above the door rang. My shoes stayed on the floor, and my heart stayed in my chest. It was a glorious day.

"What's got you smiling?" Marty leaned his cane against the table and helped Mona into the booth I'd just cleaned.

She reached over and cuffed the back of his head. "I told you she met a man last night." Mona scooted in, and Marty slid next to her. They were cute in an odd couple kind of way. Marty was gasoline, and Mona was fire, but somehow their combination wasn't combustible. Mona simply burned up Marty's fuel, and he was happy to keep her flame going.

Of all the things we talked about, Mona remembered my mention of a man. "It's meatloaf today," I said.

"Two specials and two soda pops, please." Marty always ordered for Mona. It wasn't because she couldn't see the menu. She had it memorized. It was more of a chivalrous thing. He proved he knew what she liked, and she proved that she trusted his choices. It was like a dance, where Marty had two left feet and Mona two right, but together they made a perfect pair.

A lot can be learned from watching couples interact, I reflected as I placed their order and delivered the sodas.

"Who's this man, young lady?" Marty folded his napkin into a perfect square and placed his Coke on top of it. He reached for Mona's napkin and did the same.

"A guy that needed some help. He crashed a motorcycle and cut his arm up pretty bad. I bandaged him up and sent him on his way."

"Remember what we talked about this morning?"

"I couldn't let him bleed to death at the diner door, so I put his mask on first."

Marty looked at us like we were speaking Polish.

"Hannah is a do-gooder, always fixing other people without taking care of herself."

Marty plopped a straw in his drink and then Mona's. He took care of his stuff first and then took care of hers next. I would have considered that selfish, but after Mona's airplane lecture, I saw it differently: Once a person's needs are met, they are more capable of serving others.

He turned toward Mona as if I weren't there. "I don't know if I'd call her a do-gooder, dear. She did come late to the party when Ryker and Silas were on trial."

"Oh, pish. Once she was okay, she was able to help the boys."

I left them to their argument and went to fetch their meatloaf and mash. When I got back, they both were armed and ready with their forks and knives.

"You two enjoy." I went about my cleaning duties. The floor was in good shape. Despite the storm, Dex was thorough in his mop job.

I closed my eyes and saw him. Eyes the color of a summer sky. A body as big and solid as a mountain. A liquid voice that oozed sexiness. My body shivered at the memory of him.

"Earth to Hannah," Grace's familiar voice called out.

I swung around to find her and Ana tucked into a booth with their babies, Wren and Blue. It was hard to not let the green shade of envy consume me. They had everything I wanted. They had Ryker and Silas and two adorable boys. What did I have? *Zilch.*

"You okay?" Ana asked.

Mona craned around. "She's daydreaming about some young man who showed up last night."

"After we left?" Grace asked.

Ana turned to Grace. "I told you we shouldn't have left."

"It's not like she wanted us here." They continued to argue while I grabbed the coffee pot and two cups.

"I was fine. Some guy had an accident. He used the phone and left."

The girls looked at me like a booger hung from my nose. I swiped at my face in case. "You let a strange man in after what happened to you?" Did some mothering switch flip on the minute a woman gave birth?

I poured the coffee. "It was raining, and I couldn't let him bleed all over the floor."

It was a rare moment when both Grace and Ana were silenced. They sat with their mouths open. "Blood?" they said in unison.

"What the hell were you thinking?" Grace groused. Even Blue started at the gruffness of her tone.

I slid into the booth next to Ana, pushing inch by inch until one of my butt cheeks was all the way on the bench.

"I was thinking someone needed help." I glanced at the counter I had cowered behind, remembering how my initial reaction hadn't exactly been welcoming. "It wasn't the smartest choice, but I'm glad I did it. I met a guy who wanted nothing from me but a bandage and a phone."

"He must be the owner of the motorcycle that crashed into the big oak at the end of town." Ana brushed Wren's hair from his forehead. For a two-month-old, he had a full head of dark hair. There was no questioning who his father was; Wren was a mini-me of Ryker from his dark locks, to his blue eyes, to the dimple on his chin.

"Silas and Ryker picked it up and brought it to the garage, waiting for the owner to claim it. Do you know how to reach the guy?"

I pulled my phone from my pocket. "I've got the number of the person who picked him up. I think he said his name was John." I scrolled to the number I didn't recognize, tore a page from my order pad, and scribbled it down.

"Odd that he'd leave it abandoned."

Inside, I felt an overwhelming need to defend Dex. "He was hurt, and it was raining. I'm sure he plans to come back and claim it." I tried to discipline my voice, to keep it calm and even-keeled, but the lift of Grace's brow proved I'd failed.

"Do I detect some attraction to this stranger?"

"I'm not talking about a man I don't know." I popped up from the booth. "Are you going to order or what?"

"I sense some deflection going on here, don't you, Grace?" Ana had her tell-me-the-truth face perfected. Poor Wren didn't have a chance when he grew up.

I jutted out my hip and pasted on a bored face. "So is that a no to the food?"

Grace ripped the menu from the holder. She pointed to the grilled cheese sandwich. "Fries too."

I turned toward Ana. "Soup and salad, please. Still trying to take this baby weight off my ass."

The woman looked amazing for having pushed out a kid eight weeks ago. It was another thing that pissed me off. She got the guy.

She got the baby. And I'd be damned if she didn't get her pre-baby body back. Some girls got everything. I wasn't one of them.

"Don't forget the old people." Mona held up her empty soda glass, and I went back to work. A full diner meant lots of tips, but an empty diner gave me a moment of peace. And peace was something I didn't get much of these days.

Ten minutes before my shift ended, the door opened, but I couldn't see the person's face through the flowers they were carrying.

A large vase of roses was plunked down on the counter, and the young delivery boy peeked his head around the arrangement and smiled. "Delivery for Hannah."

I turned a finger toward myself. "Me?"

"Are you Hannah?"

I spun around as if some other Hannah was hiding behind me. "I'm her…I mean, that's me."

"Then these are for you." The kid pressed a clipboard into my hands. "Sign here."

Once I signed, I handed it back, but he didn't leave. I'd never had anyone send me flowers; what the heck was he waiting for? It only took a second for my mind to function and my cheeks to redden. It had been a slow day at the diner, and I'd only made ten bucks, but I pressed half of my wrinkly bills into his palm. "Thank you."

For minutes, I stared at the red roses, smelling each one individually, trying to decide whether one smelled better than the next. My fingers brushed up their velvety petals to the card.

The flowers thrilled me and scared me. I hoped they were from Dex, but they could be from Cameron Longfellow. It was like him to take something beautiful and destroy it. His threat of seeing me soon was never far from my thoughts.

With shaking hands, I pulled the card from the tiny envelope.

You and me
Dinner
Tomorrow night
Seven o'clock
Boulder Dushanbe Teahouse
See you there, Hannah

Dex

The card fell from my hands to the checkered floor.

I had a date. A real date. With Dex Riley.

When Rosemarie arrived at the diner for her shift, I literally ran out the door. There was so much to do before tomorrow night.

Chapter 6

DECKER

Diane, the clerk at the rental agency, happily accepted my check. I was now the proud new owner of a Harley-Davidson Fat Boy. The damn thing might never run again, but it was mine.

Thank God I had my own money because I couldn't imagine asking my father for the sixteen thousand dollars it cost. Dad was already close to death, and this situation would have finished him off.

I tucked the receipt in my pocket and hurried to my Range Rover. To the average person, I looked like I had it made. I was the sole heir to a multimillion-dollar company. I was rich. I had a loving mother and a successful father. Life should have been golden, but somehow mine was tarnished.

My phone rang as I climbed into the Rover. It was John. He must have picked up my bike.

"Hey, John, did you find it next to the tree?"

"Nope, it's at The Nest. A garage owned by those brothers you met."

"The Savage brothers have my bike?" Disbelief colored my words.

"They got my number from Hannah and called to tell me they picked it up and took it to their shop."

"You're shitting me." My laughter couldn't be contained. Life was full of surprises.

"I told them you'd be in touch."

"Thanks, man. I've got it from here."

A turn of the key and the engine purred to life. First stop was The Nest. What were the chances that the brothers I met yesterday would end up with my newly purchased bike?

The forty-five-minute drive flew by because my head was full of Hannah. Had she gotten the flowers yesterday? Did she like them? Would she show for our date tonight?

When I pulled into The Nest's parking lot, Ryker and Silas were pulling my bike from the bed of their truck. I hopped out and started their way. Their eyes went from the bike to me, then to the Range Rover.

"Dude. Is this yours?" Silas yanked on the back tire and pulled the mangled heap to the tailgate edge.

Now that I saw the damage, I considered myself lucky to have survived.

They left it hanging partway off the back of the truck and walked to me.

"You walked away from this without a scratch?"

I pulled up the sleeve of my Henley and showed them Hannah's fine first-aid job. "Nope. I'm missing a few layers of skin and probably a few brain cells, but I'm mostly intact."

"You want us to try to fit it in the back end of your car?" Ryker walked around my SUV, sizing things up. "It isn't going to fit."

"I've heard you specialize in fixing Harleys."

Silas stood a bit taller like pride had lifted him an inch or two. "We do, and it looks like you could use our services. Care to tell us how you wrapped this bad boy around a tree?"

"Not really. Let's say it was a solid learning experience. Check the weather before you ride." I walked to the bike and ran my palm over the tire. "Can it be fixed?" I'd never been a quitter, and I wasn't going to let an oak tree dissuade me from my next ride.

"Everything is fixable," Ryker said. "Let's go inside. We can have a drink and talk bikes."

They led me into the garage where they offered me an upside-down bucket as a chair. I liked their style. There was something pure and honest about the way they did business. No pretense. No ten-foot conference table. No refrigerator full of Perrier.

Silas grabbed a six-pack of beer from a cooler in the corner. He pulled a can from the ring and tossed it to me. I caught it midair. It would be so easy to pop the top and relish the cold carbonation, but then I'd have to call my sponsor. He'd talk to me until two suns had risen and set, and I'd miss my date with Hannah.

"No thanks." I tossed it back. "Do you have a soda? Even water would do." I wasn't going to come out of the gate with *I have a drinking problem*. I wasn't dating these guys, merely doing business with them.

Ryker yanked the beers from Silas and shoved them back into the cooler. When he turned around, he held three bottles of water.

"You don't have to abstain because of me. I have to hit the road in a bit, and drinking and driving aren't a good combination."

Ryker looked at Silas and grinned. "He's smart."

Silas slid down the wall and sat on the concrete floor. "How long have you been working for your dad?"

"My whole life." Dad had had me wearing suits and taking notes since the day I could walk and hold a pen in my hand. There were pictures to prove my claim. Me at two sitting in his chair at the office. Me at eight drawing on a whiteboard in the conference room. Me at twelve standing in front of a sold sign. It was my first commission. Of course, I wasn't old enough to work, but the couple loved the way I showed them the finer qualities of the house through a kid's eye. They signed the contract right then, and Dad put the commission into my savings account.

The first sale was fun, but the pressure to perform was not. While most kids played T-ball, I learned about market trends.

"You like real estate?" Ryker asked. He sat on a crotch rocket and relaxed against the gas tank.

"It's a job. It pays well." Dad pressured me to step up when all I wanted to do was step down. I didn't mind the work, but I didn't find it fulfilling. Each commission wasn't the be-all and end-all to my life. I wasn't motivated by money. I'd never been without it, so it wasn't a driving force in my life. And when Dad died, I'd be in charge of Riley Realty. That alone made the acid churn in my stomach. Not only would I be responsible for my own existence, but an entire company would depend on me. That was too much damn pressure for a guy my age.

"As long as you're happy. You are happy, right?" Silas took aim and shot his bottle cap toward the steel drum in the corner. He sank his shot with ease. It was such a carefree action, and yet I didn't think I'd ever done it. From my perch on the bucket, I tried for a three-point shot and missed. The cap hit the wall and rolled to the center of the garage.

"Remind me to put him on the other team the next time we play hoops," Silas teased.

I didn't mind Silas's jab at my skills. At least it stopped me from answering the question regarding my happiness. The only time I could remember being truly happy was two nights ago when I sat in an empty diner and ate pie with a stranger. She didn't know me. She didn't judge me. She didn't want anything from me.

"What do you do for fun?" Ryker asked. He pushed off the bike and hopped up on top of an old metal table.

"Fun?" A laugh busted from my gut. I looked at the Harley in the bay next to where we sat. "I ride motorcycles."

"You suck at that too." Silas looked at Ryker. "Bro, he needs us more than he knows."

Some would be offended, but I wasn't. I did suck at riding a motorcycle. "Maybe you guys can show me a few things. What do you ride?"

The two brothers exchanged glances, and Ryker spoke. "Nothing right now. We had to sell some stuff for a family situation, but we do love our Harleys."

"You got a girl?" Silas leaned forward like he was truly interested in getting to know me. The brothers were weirdly friendly. They asked a lot of questions, but not the normal questions I usually got.

"I've had lots of girls." It was the truth. Someone like me didn't let people get close. Growing up, all I seemed to get were friends or girl-friends who were attracted to my family money, not me.

These guys, along with Hannah, didn't seem to care who I was or what I was worth. It didn't seem to influence them. They were the coolest people I'd met in a long time.

"No girlfriend?" Ryker's legs swung back and forth and beat out a rhythm on the metal legs of the table.

"Nope, but I met some chick at the diner the other night." I raised my injured arm. "She bandaged me up and fed me pie."

"The diner here in town?" Ryker asked.

I nodded. The thought of Hannah made me smile. "Hot blonde. Do you know her?"

"Hannah?" Silas's eyes grew wide.

"That's the one." I couldn't tame the racing of my heart. Odd since most girls barely affected me beyond a hard-on. "I've got a date with her tomorrow night."

The trill of my phone ended the conversation. I sighed when I looked at the screen. "It's my dad. Excuse me, I have to take his call." I stepped outside to answer. "Hello."

"I need you in the office now." The abrupt demand of my return to the office wasn't abnormal; his calls rarely started with hello.

"I'm an hour outside of town." I pulled my phone from my ear. It was three o'clock. Plenty of time to get to Boulder, get my ass chewed for some unknown infraction, and make reservations at the Dushanbe Teahouse. "See you then." I didn't give him a chance to interrogate me. That would come soon enough.

When I walked back into the garage, the brothers were wheeling in my broken bike. Handlebars bent. Spokes missing. Tank caved in. It was a mess.

"That was work. I've got to go."

They set the bike down and walked toward me. "You coming back soon?" Silas asked. "We can teach you how to ride this beast."

"I'll be back. I've tasted the pie, and I want more." They were guys and knew I was talking about more than the pastry. If things went my way, I'd get my fill of Hannah soon. If not, I'd definitely be back for her pie another day.

"HE'S IN HIS OFFICE," Rose said when I walked in. She'd been working for my dad since I could remember. "He's not in a good mood."

"What's new?" I shook my head as I walked past her desk. The long hallway to Dad's office was like the green mile. Every step forward was a step closer to misery and the death of hope and happiness.

Mom was standing in the office when I arrived. She was the glue that bound our family together. My father was hard and had a Hades-hot temper. My mother was soft and saintly.

"Mom, what are you doing here?" I pulled her in for a hug.

"I can't have my favorite men at each other's throats." She pushed me back and looked at me with the kind of love I'd only seen from her. Pure unfettered love.

I was happy to see her here, but I felt guilty too. I was a grown man and should have been able to deal with my father by myself.

I turned to my father, who held a tumbler of brown liquid. Tea it wasn't. He'd been self-medicating for years, first to numb the fact that his life was all about work, and then to numb the pain of his cancer. He was using the thing that was killing him to get through the day.

I wanted to tell him to stop with his drinking, but who was I to give advice? I'd been sober for nearly three years, but once an alcoholic, always an alcoholic. In fact, it was my father's cancer diagnosis that helped set me straight. I didn't want to be like him in any way. His blood ran through my veins, and that meant a real risk of pancreatic and liver cancer for me. There were things I couldn't change and things I could. One was staying sober. Another was making Mom happy by apologizing to Dad.

"I'm sorry, Dad. I always seem to be a disappointment, but I'll try harder." I didn't want this company, but as Rip Riley's only child, the company was my birthright and responsibility.

This was one of those times when I wished I wasn't an only child. To share the burden with another sibling would have been heaven. Too bad Mom wasn't able to have another kid after I was born. The hell it took to bring me into the world, or so I was told, made that impossible.

Dad sucked back his tumbler and grabbed for the near empty decanter. The same decanter that had been filled to the top yesterday. "Where have you been?"

"I took a ride to Fury."

"Let it go, Decker. I only let you have the meeting so you could see the difference between potential clients and poor choices. Those boys are poor choices. They have nothing to offer you."

"They're nice guys."

Dad slammed his glass on the table, splashing the liquid over the edge. "Nice doesn't pay the rent."

"Stop this, you two." Mom pulled a Kleenex from a nearby box and wiped up the spill. "Why this interest in Fury? You've never been there before." Worry creased her forehead.

I turned away from Dad's scowl. "I never had a reason to go there, and then a development opportunity came up."

"It's a dying town, I hear." Mom walked past me to throw away the wet tissue. She bumped my arm, and I silently screamed. There was no way I'd react visibly to the pain. It was enough that she was worried about Dad; I wouldn't add to her troubles.

"It's the perfect commuter town for Boulder. I met some of the residents, and I like them."

"Liking them isn't important. It doesn't affect the end game, Decker."

I ignored his comment. After a few drinks, Dad spewed nothing but vitriol.

Mom ignored him too. She took me in from head to toe, her smile warm and bright. "You look different."

"He's sober," Dad piped in.

I wanted to lash out at him. He was a shitty role model when it came to responsible drinking, but like Mom, I let it go and focused on her. Some fights weren't worth the effort.

"What do you mean I look different?" She always had that scary sixth sense that mothers had, and I wondered whether she knew I'd had an accident.

"I'm not sure yet." She cupped my cheek with motherly love. "I'll tell you when I figure it out."

Chapter 7

HANNAH

A song sang in my heart. The sun had set, but everything around me seemed bright and fresh.

Mom was in the kitchen making spaghetti. Even she seemed renewed.

"It looks like you're feeling better," I said.

She snapped her head around toward me. "No, I've got the shakes. I've puked three times today. My skin looks like I have hepatitis. And I've screwed up your life."

I set my purse on the old worn table. "Come here." I held my arms open and waited for her to walk into them, and she did. "You can do this, Mom." I gave her a long, hard squeeze.

The truth was, she could generally do a few days. She was always remorseful when sober and angry when she slipped back into old habits.

Mom pushed away and went back to the stove where she dumped a package of pasta into the boiling water.

"What's got you looking so happy?" She stirred the spaghetti until it wilted into the water.

I glanced at my reflection in the window. My eyes were no longer puffy, and there was some pink to my cheeks. "Wait here." I raced to my car to grab the flowers. It had been a long time since flowers sat in the middle of our table. I turned them around to see whether there was a better, fuller side, but the vase was beautiful from every angle.

"You brought me flowers?" Mom's eyes lit up, and her face brightened with a smile. Happiness looked good on her.

"I'm sharing my flowers with you." I leaned in and sniffed at the beautiful blooms.

Mom turned back to stir the sauce. "Who are they from?"

I told her the story of Dex coming into the diner injured. "He's super nice and cute."

"The not-so-bright one that crashed in the rain?" She gave me a haven't-you-learned-anything look. "At least he has some class, but remember, after the flowers always comes heartbreak."

"Not all men are bad, Mom." It took a lot for me to say that because lately, my jerk-to-nice ratio was tipping toward jerk. "Just because you found the one tarnished penny in the bunch doesn't mean you shouldn't keep looking for the shiny coin."

"Where do you come up with that stuff? Last week you told me I was a couch potato in the gravy boat of life."

I was surprised she remembered. "I like metaphors."

"Okay, but you're the only one who understands what in the hell you're saying."

"Not true." The legs of the chair scraped across the linoleum floor and creaked when I took a seat. "All I was saying was, spending your day on the couch is not productive. It doesn't make your life any better."

Mom pounded the sauce spoon on the counter, sending a splatter of red specks onto the dingy white wall. "My life is over. All I have is Judge Judy and carbohydrates."

This was where it all began. First the moment of sober reflection, followed by the pity party, chased by a bottle of hard liquor, and then concluding with whatever pain pills she could wrangle from her doctor.

"Do you blame me?" It was a question I asked myself all the time. Could I have done something different? I had a look that men gravitated to. Many girls would consider that a blessing. For me, it had been a curse until I figured out how to use it. Then it became a cata-strophe because flirting was different from consent.

Mom reached into the cabinet above the stove. I held my breath and prayed she wouldn't drag down a bottle. Work was tiring enough, but the daily searches and seizures were exhausting. At some point in the past year, I'd become the parent, and I was completely unqualified.

I exhaled loudly when I saw the colander. Could it be that things were finally looking up?

"I have a date tomorrow night."

She turned and focused on the flowers. "With the diner boy?"

"Yes. His name is Dex."

"Where's he taking you?" This was my old mom sneaking past the fog.

I rose and grabbed two plates from the cupboard. "I'm meeting him at the Dushanbe Teahouse in Boulder." I dished up the drained spaghetti, and Mom dumped a scoop of sauce on each plate. We plopped into opposite seats at the table.

Her brows lifted, and I waited for the smile that never came. "He can't pick you up?"

I thought she'd be excited that I met someone, but instead, she fixated on a meaningless detail. "He works in Boulder, and it makes sense to meet him there." There was no way I'd let her lack of excite-ment ruin my date. The Dushanbe Teahouse was a super cool place to go and not someplace I could afford on my own.

"Don't settle, Hannah. Expect more and get more." It was good advice if I'd actually seen it applied, but Mom was a do-as-I-say, not-as-I-do person.

"You should get out more. Maybe date."

She twirled the pasta around her fork. "The last time I dated, it didn't work out well for you."

"He didn't rape me, Mom. He …"

"Hannah, please don't say it. I can't bear it." She dropped her fork and pulled her hands to her ears. "I was supposed to protect you. It was my job to make sure you were safe."

I hated it when she played the martyr. She lowered her hands when I swatted at them. "You know what, Mom? Stop being the damn victim. I'm the one that got touched by the asshole. You're the one that stopped him. You *did* protect me, and then you shut down and gave up."

"I lost my job." She shoved her plate forward as if she were finished after the first bite.

"Yes, you did, but you could do something else. It's not my dream to schlep plates and pour coffee, but it puts pasta on the table." I shoved her plate back toward her. "Eat before you have bigger problems than a pickled liver and a bad attitude." I wanted to crawl under the table and hide. I was often snarky, but I was rarely disrespectful to my elders.

"Your mouth is going to get you into trouble."

"It already has." It was my mouthing off at Cameron that got me a fist to the face, or so he'd claimed. That purple cheek had gone unnoticed by Mom because she'd been in a particularly low place. Drunk and passed out on the carpet for days, to be specific.

"I can't stay here and take care of you forever. I have dreams too, Mom."

"Then leave."

These were the times I wanted to throw my hands in the air and scream that I quit, but I couldn't quit on the ones I loved. "That's not what families do. You fought for me, I'll fight for you, but you have to fight for yourself too. No more booze or pills. When you feel desperate, take a walk or come to the diner and have some pie."

"You can't make enough pie to fill my desperate moments."

"Maybe not. All I know is that you have to find something else to fill your void."

"You quit school for me. What's filling your void?" But she went back to eating, which was a victory.

"I work, I have friends, and now I have a date." After thinking I would never find the right guy, I was finally filled with hope.

A loud thud came from the front door. When I opened it, I found my sister standing on the stoop with tears in her eyes.

"I lost my key," she cried.

I was shocked to see Stacey standing in front of me. She was supposed to be cramming for her finals, not knocking at the door.

"What the hell are you doing here?" I stepped aside so she could enter.

Stacey yanked a big duffle through the door and plopped it in the middle of the living room.

It wasn't the type of bag someone brought for a short stay. She was back for good.

"I'm homesick."

My intuition told me there was a story behind her sudden appearance and far more to it than those two simple words. "What's going on, Stacey?"

She pulled me in for a hug. "Nothing, I just miss you guys." She held her nose high. "Is that spaghetti I smell?" And she was off to the kitchen. Stacey had the evasion techniques of a ninja and the stubbornness of a bull.

Chapter 8

HANNAH

The damn owl clock didn't move fast enough. I'd checked it a dozen times, and the hour still hadn't passed. My throat vibrated with a growl.

The door chimed, and in walked the gang minus Mona and Marty. When it was all six of them together, they piled into the big corner booth. Today they took up the smaller table in the center of the diner.

"It's French toast Friday," Ana said with joy bubbling from her pores.

I brought both pots of coffee to the table: decaf for the breast-feeding Ana and fully loaded for everyone else.

"Are you all having the special?"

"Yes," Ryker said. "Can you put in the order and come back? There's something I need to talk to you about."

Once I slapped the order onto the wheel at the kitchen window, I returned to the table. I had no idea what he wanted to talk about. Maybe he was going to yell at me for leaving alone at night too. I'd never had a big brother, and since I'd had a major crush on Ryker, I certainly didn't want him to take on that role. Honestly, it was hard to look at him as anything but a disappointment.

He pulled a chair from a nearby table and slid it toward the group. Anything that required I sit down couldn't be good. I plunked my butt into the seat and waited for them to ruin my day.

They all looked at me like I'd grown a horn out of my forehead.

Grace broke the silence. "That guy you met the other night here…the one who crashed his bike?" She scanned the crowd in the booth. "Well…that's Decker."

My head turned from side to side while I analyzed everyone's expressions. Silas and Ryker waited silently for a reaction. The girls gave me an are-you-dense look.

"Wait." I leaned forward and elbowed the table. "Do you mean your Decker, as in your long-lost brother?" It couldn't be. He was so different from Silas and Ryker. To start a list of dissimilarities, he was nice, and he was put together in a way they could never be. "He said his name was … oh, my God. His name is Dex." He'd obviously flown under their radar by using that name.

I reflected back on Wednesday night, trying to bring his image into my mind. I looked at the brothers. "He has the Savage eyes."

Ryker ignored my observation. He was on a mission, and Ryker never strayed when he was focused. "We set up a meeting. Never expected he'd come to town to check the place out in advance."

"He's a Savage. He pays attention to details," Silas added.

The brothers argued a minute over who Decker favored and discussed what attributes were definitely Savage-born ones. The girls chatted about the good and bad traits he might have. I got dizzy trying to follow the conversations.

I cleared my throat. "As much as I'd like to sit here while you argue over your brother, I can't. What do you need to talk to me about?"

"Right." Ryker laid his hand on my shoulder. The man hadn't ever touched me, except that one time he pushed me from the booth and I landed flat on my ass on the hard tile floor, and in a way, this gentle touch was as shocking and forceful. "I need you to help us."

I sat back, forcing his hand to drop away. "What do you want from me?"

Ryker and Silas whispered back and forth, but it was Silas who spoke up. "We tracked him to a business in Boulder. We went to talk to his family firm about finding a broker to finance the development of Fury. We were feeling him out." Silas's voice cracked, and he took a sip of coffee.

"And?" They still hadn't told me what they wanted, but it was my experience that anything needing a long lead-in was never good.

"We don't think he knows he's adopted."

I slid back, making the metal legs of the chair screech against the floor. "And you want me to tell him?"

Ryker rolled his eyes. "No. That's not what we want. We just want you to feel him out," he said. "We don't know what to do next. I want to tell him, but Silas believes that if Decker is happy, maybe we should let him be and not disrupt his life. So I want to know if he's happy. I want to know if he's better off where he is. Will you do that for me?"

Ryker stared at me with those Savage blue eyes. All three men had them, and months ago their appeal might have worked on me, but after the Cameron incident, I was cautious. Especially when men asked anything of me. Maybe overly so, but I didn't want to get pulled into any more messes.

"Order up," the cook called. I pushed the chair into its place by the nearby table and rushed to claim the four specials.

I never gave Ryker an answer, and I wasn't sure that I would. I knew how important family was, and I wanted to help him, but what he was asking me to do didn't feel right. It was kind of like lying by omission. I knew something about Decker that he didn't know about himself. Was it my place to enlighten him?

For the next hour, I fussed over the counter and stayed far away from the Savages in the corner. When they left, Ryker approached me alone. "He told us about your date. I'm not asking you to sneak into his bank account or take photos of his contact list. This isn't espionage. I want to know if he's in a good place in his life. Okay?"

The sincerity in those damn blue eyes melted my resistance. I nodded my head. What choice did I have? I was going on this date to have fun and get to know the man. If, along the way, he told me he was happy, what harm would it do to share that with my friends?

I'd keep what I knew about Decker to myself. If I came clean about the truth, it would be like dropping a bomb on our date. I wasn't ready to destroy what I hadn't had a chance to create. I had no choice but to keep my mouth shut.

DID BEING anxious mean I was excited…or fearful? I tried to calm my racing heart as I pulled onto Thirteenth Street into the one remaining parking spot. That seemed lucky even though the street name sounded like a bad omen.

I yanked down the sun visor and looked into the mirror at my bloodshot eyes. I hadn't slept much last night, thinking of seeing Decker again. This was my first real date in a long time. But was it a date? The invitation sat on the passenger seat next to me. Nowhere did it say date. Had I misinterpreted his meaning? Maybe this was simply a thank you for letting him in.

That would be ironic, since the truth was, I'd let him into more than the diner. I let him into my head. The damn man consumed my thoughts. No one else had been able to break past my protective barriers, but he did. I'd been wrapped in yellow caution tape since that day in the diner parking lot. The tight grip of fear seemed to evaporate the minute I opened the door to the possibility of something with Decker.

When I arrived at the hostess stand, Decker wasn't anywhere in sight. The woman offered to seat me since there was a reservation under his last name, but I declined. I preferred to wait and be seated together.

The interior was beautiful. Intricately painted columns held up a work-of-art ceiling. While I waited, I read the history of the building. The Teahouse was constructed in Dushanbe, Tajikistan. It was a gift to Boulder to serve as a symbol of friendship. Which seemed the perfect place to get to know Decker.

I felt him before I saw him. The air crackled with energy. Dressed in a pair of black jeans and a matching long-sleeved cotton shirt, he looked more bad boy than boardroom.

In the time it took him to reach me, I second-guessed everything from my dress to my lip-gloss.

"You came." He said it like he expected me to be a no-show. Was he insane?

"You invited me. Of course, I came." It was hard to pull my eyes from his face, but I forced them to his injured arm. "How's the road rash?"

"You were right. It hurt like hell yesterday, but it's better today. I changed the bandage. Not pretty to look at, but it's healing." He placed his palm on the small of my back and led me the few feet to the hostess stand.

The girl behind the podium lit up like a street lamp, but her smile was for him only. "Decker, it's so good to see you again. Do you want your normal table?" She slowly turned her feline face to me, and I swore invisible claws gouged out my eyes.

Decker's whole demeanor changed. His hand dropped to his side. An immediate frost chilled the surrounding air. "Cancel the reservations," he snapped.

The catty chick at the stand stood with her mouth hanging open. "But you always—"

"Cancel it." His voice resonated through the entry.

I stared up at him, and our eyes met. "I shouldn't have done this." He shook his head, gripped my elbow, and nearly dragged me outside.

My stomach clenched as he walked too fast for me to keep up in heels. I pulled free from his grasp and stopped on the sidewalk. "If you wanted to back out, I wish you'd have told me before I drove all this way to see you."

"It's not that," he said, his frown flipping to a smile. "You've got it all wrong."

Chapter 9

DECKER

Old habits are hard to break, but Hannah deserved better. The minute the hostess said hello, I realized what a mistake I'd made.

Standing in the middle of the sidewalk, I reached for her hands. She eyed me warily before she let me hold them. "I want tonight to be special." I looked toward the restaurant entrance. "That place isn't special."

She looked over her shoulder toward the door. "It seemed pretty special to me."

"It's okay, but it's not for you." I wrapped my arm around her shoulder and moved her toward my SUV. "Trust me?" I could see the uncertainty in her eyes. I couldn't blame her for putting her guard up. So far I had a pretty bad track record with this girl.

"Trust isn't something I give easily."

"I promise to earn yours." I opened the door to the passenger side of the Range Rover and helped Hannah inside. "I want to take you somewhere that is special to me. Someplace I've never shared with anyone."

The skepticism in her pale blue eyes was replaced by a glint of happiness.

When I climbed into the driver's seat, she asked, "Is this *your* car?" She turned in the seat to look behind her.

Thankfully I'd had it detailed this morning. My normal collection of coffee cups and candy wrappers was gone.

"Yes, well, it's actually a company car."

"You said you work for a broker, right?"

I couldn't believe she still didn't know who I was. There were few in this world that didn't know what being Rip Riley's son meant. It was such a thrill to be out with a girl who didn't know who I was or what I had.

"Yes, I work for my father. He's a broker, and I'm a real estate agent working on my broker license."

"Is that why you didn't want to take me to Dushanbe? Is that where you take your clients?"

How did I tell her the truth? There was something real and pure about Hannah that attracted me. She showed me her vulnerabilities as well as her big-heartedness. I wanted to see where we could take this new relationship. I knew it would not survive if we started it with a thread of dishonesty.

I lowered my voice as if someone else besides us could hear my shame. "No. It's where I take all my dates, and you deserve something better." I waited for her to lash out the way most girls would, but she didn't. She sat back and stared out the window.

"Do you prefer Decker or Dex? I've heard both."

"I answer to both, so whatever works." My friends called me Dex, but I liked the way my given name rolled off her tongue. "About the restaurant, are you angry at me?"

She certainly had a right to be. I'd invited her to a specific place, and like a crazy, possessed lunatic, I shoved her into my car and took off in another direction.

She shifted her body to face me. The smell of her perfume or lotion or shampoo wafted through the air. She smelled like fresh-picked strawberries.

"Angry...no. Curious...yes." She rested her head against the seat back, her blonde hair a stark contrast to the black leather interior. "So you have a lot of first dates?"

I wanted to reach into my mouth and rip out my tongue or dig farther back and extract my vocal cords so nothing else could come out of my mouth.

"I'm not proud to say I've had my share of first dates. What I can say is, I've never been as excited to go on a date as I am for this one."

A soft lilting giggle filled the interior. "I bet you say that to all the girls."

"Not true." I turned onto the highway and headed toward Golden. "Can I confess something to you?" I asked. A quick glance in her direction was rewarded with her smile.

"It's only our first date. Are you sure we're ready for confessions? Maybe we should find a priest or someone better suited to listen to your sins."

"I'm pretty sure what I have to say doesn't fall into the sin category. Not yet anyway." I'd had some pretty sinful visions of Hannah already. Hannah naked. Hannah naked and riding me. Hannah and those full pink lips sucking me into her mouth.

I shook those thoughts from my head. "That conversation we had back in the diner—I've never done that before. I've never known a girl who didn't want something from me. You don't even know who I am, let alone that I have everything I do." I pulled into the parking lot of a hole-in-the-wall called The Dive and killed the engine. "I could be wrong, but I get the feeling that none of that matters to you."

"Who are you?" She looked at me like I was a puzzle. Like somehow I was a piece she couldn't find a place for. I hoped I could change her mind.

I shrugged. "I'm Decker. The guy who can't ride a motorcycle or stop stepping on his tongue." I opened the door and raced to her side of the Rover. When I opened it, I said, "Give me a chance."

She hopped out and offered her hand. I supposed that was her way of saying yes.

"Where are we?" She looked left and right at what seemed the most unlikely place to take a date.

"My favorite place in the world." And I wanted to share it with her. "You'll be the first woman I've ever brought here."

She read the sign and laughed. "It's a real dive."

"The sign doesn't lie, but it's the hole-in-the-wall places that are the best."

"I don't know. The Diner is a dive, but it's the only gig in town, so no one has much choice."

I set my hand on her lower back and walked her to the door. "The pie was good. The company was better."

"Are you flirting with me?"

"Is it working?" When the door opened, the smell of savory dishes floated past us.

"Yes, it's kind of working." She stopped in the doorway. "Although I was excited to go to Dushanbe. I'd never been there, and I love tea."

"I'll make it up to you." The place had open seating, and I scoped out a private table in the corner. I wanted to share this place with Hannah, but I didn't want to share Hannah with anyone else.

"Does that mean we'll have a second date?" She took a seat, and I pulled a chair next to her.

"There is no doubt in my mind." Hannah was a cool girl, a real girl who probably wouldn't fit in with the stuffy people my father would have me surround myself with … and that was fine by me. Hannah made me feel like I could be myself.

A shadow crossed the table. "Decker, how's it going?" Tanner walked up to me and slapped me on the back, but his eyes were on Hannah. "Who do we have here?" Even though my best friend was old enough to be her father, a bolt of jealousy surged through me. I didn't want anyone to look at Hannah. As far as I was concerned, she was already mine.

"Tanner, this is *my* date, Hannah." Her hand sat on the table, and I covered it with mine. It was a total caveman move to claim her, but it didn't seem to bother her. In fact, her smile bloomed.

"Nice to meet you." She gave him a cursory glance and turned her attention back to me. My chest swelled, knowing she had eyes only for me.

"You want the regular?" Tanner asked. His brows lifted to disappear under his bangs.

"Yep, bring us two. Hannah's decided to give me a chance." I leaned back and took a look around the place. It was everything I needed it to be. Comfortable and down to earth.

"He's a smart bet."

"Are you?" Hannah asked.

I left my hand over hers because it felt right. "A smart bet? It depends on who you talk to."

Tanner leaned over the table like he was telling a secret. "I wouldn't have any of this without him. Kind of amazing considering how we met." He turned and walked back to the kitchen, leaving me alone to explain.

"What does that mean?"

It was times like these when the world felt like it was crashing down on me. One moment I had something good within my grasp, and the next it might be gone.

I stared into Hannah's eyes. Blue pools full of concern and compassion looked back at me. She'd left school for something or someone. Something told me she had a story to tell, and it might be worse than mine. I thought about the twelve steps I'd traveled to get this place—a place of truth, perseverance, and forgiveness.

"It means I have something I need to tell you."

Chapter 10

HANNAH

I pulled my hand out from under his. It had felt so nice until the moment his words raced through my head like a greyhound chasing a rabbit. Nipping at my hope of ever finding a decent guy.

When someone started off by saying *I need to tell you something*, it never ended well. And here I was, trapped with this man who was probably going to tell me he was the baby daddy of a dozen kids. I mean, he did 'fess up to having a lot of first dates.

When I'd thought karma was going to stop being a stubborn vindictive bitch, she slapped me upside my head again.

I straightened to my full, seated height, which was roughly collarbone level to Decker. "I guess I'm ready." It wasn't like I had much choice. He'd driven. I was stuck listening to whatever he said until he drove me back or I caught a cab I couldn't afford.

He laughed like somehow destroying my dreams was funny. "I'm not a criminal."

"A criminal I can handle, just don't tell me you're married or you have a horde of kids shoved in the back of your Rover waiting for leftovers."

At the mention of leftovers, Tanner appeared with our plates. Another perfectly timed distraction.

"What we have here is what we call the Dexner. It's an open-faced burger drowned in green chili and cheese." He pushed two sodas in front of us. "You'll need this to put out the five-alarm fire."

Tanner disappeared. Decker reached out and took my hand, ignoring the food that sat in front of us. His touch was distracting, and maybe that was his plan. If I wasn't paying attention, maybe I'd miss the part where he told me he boiled people and made them into green chili for this meal.

His thumbs brushed over my knuckles, and a ribbon of heat wrapped around my traitorous body.

He cleared his throat as if making room for words. "I asked you to trust me, but I haven't been completely honest. Not because I intended to keep anything from you, but because I wanted to tell you in a place where I found strength and comfort."

"Am I going to have to call a cab?"

"I hope not."

I picked up my fork and cut off the tiniest bite. The flavors burst on my tongue. "Oh, my God, this is so good. It might be worth hearing you're a serial killer just to have tasted this meal." I slapped my hand over my mouth. "I didn't mean for that to come out."

Decker's eyes were as wide as a picture window. "I told you I wasn't a criminal."

I took a sip of the soda to cut the heat. "Neither was Hannibal Lecter until he was caught."

Decker laughed so hard he doubled over. "You are the most amazing woman I've met. I'm about to tell you something that could be a deal-breaker, and you tell a joke."

"I always joke when I'm nervous." I took another bite to keep my mouth busy, so I didn't blurt out anything else.

"I'm an alcoholic and an addict." He lowered his head as if the shame was too heavy to bear.

I tossed my fork to the table. "Seriously?" Decker looked like such a put-together guy. Still, I was relieved that this was his big confession; I'd become a regular Addicts-Are-Us representative, with my first client being my mother.

"Part of my recovery is to be honest with myself and those around me."

"I was certain you'd tell me you had a harem or something worse." I wrapped my arms around his neck and gave him a hug.

He pulled back enough to look into my face. "I told you I'm an addict, and you hugged me. What's that about?"

"Addicts need love too." I cupped his face and let my fingers linger over the dark shadow of scruff. "I can handle addiction. I do every day of my life. What I can't handle is abuse. Physical. Verbal. It's all a non-starter for me."

His fingers brushed through my hair. "Are you an addict too?" Sadness dulled his soft blue eyes.

I shook my head. "No, my mother is. I left school to take care of her."

He leaned in and brushed his lips against mine. It wasn't meant to be sexual, but supportive, and I appreciated it.

"I'm so sorry, but I can probably help. I've been there. Has she been to a program? Does she have a sponsor?" There was so much sincerity in his words.

"No, she's a self-help girl that's failing miserably, and I feel like I'm failing too."

He pressed his forehead to mine. "You can't make her stop. She has to want that for herself."

I wanted him to kiss me again, but I also wanted to hear more of his story, and the need to listen was stronger than anything else.

"Enough about me. Tell me your story."

His eyes held mine for a long minute. Every disappointment. Every pain. Every sorrow. They all shone like beacons in the depth of his eyes. "I don't know where it began." He forked a bite of his meal and savored it slowly. "For as long as I can remember, I've felt out of place." He talked between bites, and I watched him. The way his body moved with each emotion. The thick set of his lips. The stiffness in his shoulders.

"I know what that feels like. I don't fit in many places." My gut twisted at the honesty in that statement. I'd always felt like the left shoe on a right foot.

"You're perfect. You fit right here next to me. I knew it that night at the diner."

How was it that this guy who was everything I shouldn't like could say the right things and make me like him? "You're flirting again. I think your sober partner would call that deflection."

"We can ask him." He raised his hand to get Tanner's attention.

I swatted his hand down, not wanting anyone else to join us. "Later. Tell me your story."

Decker pushed his half-eaten plate away and leaned back. He never let go of my hand. It was like he needed my touch for support. "It's like I don't belong where I am," he sighed. "Like I'm living in the wrong skin. If that even makes any sense."

"More than you know." I twirled the melted cheese around my fork and plopped it into my mouth.

His eyes drifted to the bar where Tanner fixed drinks. "Tanner saved my life, and in return, I financed The Dive. It's the best non-alcoholic bar around."

I took in the surrounding room. It did seem to resemble a tavern. There was the typical wooden bar and stools, but behind it was a selection of soda that couldn't be rivaled. Drinks from Bubble Up to Seven Up and everything in between. The place was packed, and not one alcoholic beverage was being served. I hadn't noticed that until he pointed it out.

"You financed this place?" I knew enough to know that a place like this took some cash. "How did you come up with the money?"

"I'm good at selling property." The words came out indifferent. Emotionally vacant.

"I'm going to have to bring my mother here." She didn't go out much because she was usually drunk or stoned, but when she had sober days, she didn't venture out because the temptation was too strong. "It's a safe place."

Decker smiled. "This place is home." He finished his drink and paid our bill. "Are you ready to go?"

I was ready to leave the restaurant, but not ready to leave Decker. He'd been honest with me, and I'd be honest with him and tell him the truth. It might not be my place to do so, and it might be hard to hear, but this man was obviously in pain. I couldn't stand the idea of there being a place in the world that would embrace him, and him not knowing about it.

"Can we take a walk? I have something to tell you."

"Is this where you kidnap me and hold me for ransom?"

"Are you worth that much?"

"You have no idea."

I threaded my fingers through his. "No, I don't, and I don't care."

We walked along the footpath that wound through the woods behind The Dive. Since Decker was part owner and a regular visitor, he clearly knew the place like it was his backyard.

"Tell me your story," he said.

My story was not the reason that I asked for the walk and for more time. It was his story that needed to be told. His truth needed to be set free, but if he was going to be honest with me, I'd need to be honest with him.

"You know my mom's an addict. You know I dropped out of school."

"You shouldn't have done that." The fallen pine needles absorbed the sound of our footsteps, and we walked silently forward. "Your mom has to come to terms with her life, and you have to live yours."

"My mom wasn't the only one to consider. I have a sister. Stacey is in college too. I couldn't let my mom be homeless, and I couldn't ask Stacey to drop out and help me. One of us deserves a good life."

"You can both have a good life." He stopped and turned toward me. "I know it sounds selfish, but sometimes you need to take care of yourself first."

Those were Mona's words delivered differently. "I've been a selfish person more times than not. I'm trying to be a better person, but most of the time I feel like a side character in a story where everyone but me gets to live the lives they want."

His hands went to my shoulders. His lips covered my mouth. At the first touch, I was lost, consumed by a fire that skittered along my nerve endings. My heart rate climbed as the kiss heated and deepened. There was one soaring moment of bliss before he pulled back. It was a heart-stopping plunge from the highest mountain peak.

"Wow," he said. "I could do that all day."

A tingle spread from my lips throughout my body. Decker was the paddle that held the exact voltage to bring my love-dead heart back to life.

"If all your kisses are like that, I'd let you."

We held hands and walked farther along the path. The earthy smell from the recent rain and Decker's cologne filled the air. A perfect heady mix of man blended with nature. Visions of us lying in the fallen leaves with his body on top of mine heated my insides. Thoughts of his lips and tongue trailing over my skin puckered my nipples.

"Was that all you wanted to tell me?" His question was an ice bath to my arousal.

"No, I wanted you to know——"

His phone rang. He pulled it from his pocket and growled, "I have to take this."

"What's up, John?" Muffled words filled the surrounding silence. "Is this it?" Worry was etched in each line of his brow. "I'm thirty minutes away. I'll come right now."

Chapter 11

DECKER

"I 'll give you money for a cab once we get there." I rushed Hannah out of the woods and into my car without a word. Only when I was racing toward Boulder did I explain. "My dad is dying." My hands gripped the steering wheel so tight my knuckles turned white. "They've taken him to the hospital because he's in liver failure."

She reached over, pried one of my hands loose from the steering wheel, and held it in her warm palm.

"I'm so sorry, Decker. What can I do?"

"Nothing, Hannah." She didn't deserve the sharpness in my voice, and I softened my tone slightly. "I know it's in your nature to fix things. You can't fix this."

"No, but I can stay and support you."

"Don't waste your time." I was spiraling into a dangerous place where I pushed back and away to become an island. Erected the walls. Put up the barbed-wire fences. Drank myself into numbness.

"You're not a waste of time."

My head snapped in her direction in time to see her mouth stretch into a thin line.

"You don't know what I am," I said with less anger and more resignation. "But I do, and I'm probably a waste of your time."

"I should get to choose," she murmured loud enough for me to hear.

The silence following swallowed us. The closer we got to Boulder, the tighter my chest felt. The weight of a thousand failures pressed down to suffocate me. This whole date was a mistake. I liked Hannah —a lot—but I didn't deserve her. She needed someone who could be there, and that wasn't me. My entire life after Dad's death was already mapped out, and it didn't have room for a blonde slip of a girl with big blue eyes and kisses that could bring me to my knees.

I swallowed several times to soothe my sandpapered throat.

The glow of the harvest moon hid behind the clouds and cloaked the once bright sky with darkness. A single parking space sat open as if waiting for me. I pulled to a stop. The engine cut, and I took off with Hannah chasing after me.

The scent of antiseptic and death assaulted me the moment I entered the lobby. John sat in an industrial blue chair, weariness etched in his drawn, pale face.

"It doesn't look good," he said. He rubbed at the shadow of whiskers on his face.

An employee of Riley Realty, John had been around longer than I had. It had occurred to me more than once that the man Dad depended on for everything made a better son than I. John never disappointed anyone. He was born to serve, and I was born to sever. How funny that the same letters could be used to create such differing meanings.

"Is he going to die?" I asked.

John's silence told me more than his words could. Dad wouldn't walk outside again. He wouldn't inhale the scent of freshly mowed grass. Smell the crisp first snow. Feel my mother's lips against his.

A hand rubbed lightly at my back. "Everything will be okay." Hannah leaned against me, and I wrapped my arm around her shoulders.

"Nothing will ever be okay." She had no idea the turn my life would take the minute Rip Riley took his last breath.

I reached for my money-fattened wallet. Money I'd made selling the properties Dad demanded. His words galloped through my brain: *In the end, son, he who has the most, wins.* I wondered whether he felt the same now. Dad had everything. He had money and property and a devoted woman by his side, but money couldn't stop death. Would he trade it all for one more day? Probably, but he'd use that time to make more money. That was his way.

John interrupted my thoughts. "You should go to him. Hannah can stay with me. It's family only."

I pulled several twenties from my wallet and folded them into Hannah's palm. "Call a cab. There's no reason for you to stay here."

She opened her mouth to respond. The little I knew of Hannah told me she'd argue and want to stay, so I spun around and walked toward the ICU.

I inched toward the room that had *Riley* written on the dry-erase board. Mom sat in a chair next to Dad. Her teeth worried the flesh of her bottom lip. Her hands cradled one of his.

He lay like a corpse wired for sound. His skin took on the look of a spray tan gone bad. Machines chirped and bleated nonstop. Colors flashed across the screen like a video game on steroids, but there would be no winner here.

"Decker, you're here." The calmness in her voice didn't deceive me. The dullness of her eyes told me everything. A piece of her was dying with my father.

She leaned forward and tucked the bed sheet below Dad's chin. "They gave him something for the pain. He's been sleeping ever since."

I dropped to my knees in front of her. In this position, we were face to face. She'd aged twenty years in the past one. All her worry had been kept inside because Rip Riley allowed no weakness and wanted no pity. Mother suffered alone because, like my father, she was stubborn. She refused to burden anyone with her woes. The woman in front of me was a fixer like Hannah. She took care of everyone and asked for nothing in return.

"How are you, Mom?"

She smoothed the wrinkles from her skirt. "I'm fine, honey."

"You're not fine." I rose to my feet and yanked a chair to her side.

When I sat, the wooden legs creaked under my weight. "You don't have to plaster on a face for me. I'm your son."

She mothered my hand with a pat. "This was inevitable." She looked at my father and shook her head. "Stubborn man."

"I'd say it's a family trait, threaded through our DNA." We sat without words. The only sound was the constant beeping of machines that ate at my nerves.

"I've been a huge disappointment to him," I finally said.

"He loves you, Decker."

"He has a funny way of showing it." I wanted to yell and scream at the unfairness of life. How could I be born into a family with everything and feel so empty?

"He showed it the only way he knew how. He took his weaknesses and turned them into your strengths." Tears collected in her eyes. A tilt of her head sent them back from where they came.

Dad stirred, and a weak cry left his lips. He opened his yellowed eyes and gave me a sad smile. "Decker," he groaned.

I leaned forward to hear him better. Gone was the hardness normally fixed to his expression. In its place was gut-twisting pain suppressed with a half smile.

"I have to tell you something."

Was this the moment where he'd tell me he loved me? The moment when he'd say I'd been a good son? By all accounts, I'd inherited his virtues and vices. I was strong and determined but weak when it came to substances. If we measured apples to apples, I'd succeeded where he'd failed. He drank himself to death, and I'd sobered myself up to live. Maybe he'd finally acknowledge my successes rather than focusing on my failures.

I leaned in closer, making sure I didn't miss a single word.

Rasping for each breath, he said, "The Conlin contract isn't finished. You need to get the closing documents to the bank by nine."

His words hung in the air like shards of glass ready to pierce my heart. All he cared about was work.

"Honey." Mom brushed the sweaty hair from Dad's forehead. "This isn't the time to talk about contracts. Don't you have anything else you want to tell Decker?"

His face turned from hers and zeroed in on mine. "Don't look at me like I'm dead. I'm not going until I'm sure you're not going to run the business into the ground. This is your time to prove yourself. I know you have it in you."

Sad but not surprising that some of his final words were about work. Sadder yet that they were the most positive thing he'd said to me in years. On the surface, they were proof that he believed in my ability to succeed. But underneath those words were the ones he wanted to say. The ones I heard in my head all the time: *Don't screw this up.*

I couldn't take Dad's pain away. I couldn't cure his cancer. But I could allay his fears about the company. His last days on earth didn't need to be stress filled. I alone held the power to make it so. I hated real estate, but I'd learn to love it if it made Dad's final days easier. Right then, I made a pledge to be more the type of son my father wanted and needed me to be, even if it killed me.

I swallowed my regret and stood tall, shaking the weight of his disappointment from my shoulders. "I've got it." A fake smile spread across my lips as acid flooded my gut.

My lips pressed to my mom's cheek. "I'll see you both tomorrow." I left the room with my head held high and my back as stiff as rebar. Hopefully, there would be a tomorrow.

Chapter 12

HANNAH

Decker walked away and left me with John. "You're the driver, right?" I plopped in the chair next to him and let out a long sigh.

"That is but one of my duties."

"You knew my name."

John turned to face me. "Knowing things is another one of my duties."

I twisted my neck. "Are you like a spy? A bodyguard?" For an older man, he was in prime shape. Not sexy shape like Decker, but mafia hit-man shape.

John's laugh rumbled through his broad chest. "No, I've never offed anyone…yet. I'm an everything guy."

I nibbled at the hangnail on my thumb. "Decker called you from the diner the night he crashed. Are you on call all the time?"

John stretched his long legs out in front of him and leaned back, crossing his arms behind his head. "I've been with the Rileys since I was a kid. Back when they had none of their own."

"Oh, wow, so you came before Decker?"

"I was here before Decker was even a possibility." John let his arms fall and rolled to his feet. "I'm going to check on the family. You should catch that cab." He disappeared down the long bright corridor.

Everyone kept trying to push me away, but I had no place to go. I wasn't ready to deal with another drunken night with Mom, and Stacey was a whole other set of obstacles. She was in the middle of finals and should be in her dorm with her face shoved in a book. Instead, she was home for a visit with a duffle bag that I was positive held every piece of clothing she owned. Then again, that was Stacey's mode of operation. She'd always been an all-or-nothing girl.

Like John, I was restless. I wandered the hallways until I came upon the nursery. Eight bundles were nestled in acrylic bassinets behind the window. Five girls and three boys all wrapped tight like burritos.

What were their parents like? Were they loving and caring? Wasn't that how all parents began, with the best intentions and the worst outcomes?

My mind filled with visions of my future family. I wanted it all from the white picket fence to the husband and the two-point-five children, but I was a realist. I'd probably spend my life schlepping blue-plate specials and coming home to soak my bunions and rub the aching varicose veins on my legs. Life hadn't been too generous with me.

On my way back to the waiting room, I found the vending machines. I punched B-3 for M&Ms and slid over to the coffee vending machine and punched E-7 for tea. Boy had this evening turned out different from what I'd planned.

I was supposed to be sipping Moroccan Mint tea at Dushanbe while I ate lamb kabobs and couscous and looked at Decker's beautiful face. Instead, I was pulling a cup of generic tea from a machine, staring at matching white walls and floors, and breathing in the scent of sorrow that seemed to fill hospitals. Life sucked sometimes. I turned down the ER corridor on my way back to the waiting room.

Suddenly the emergency doors swung open, and the hallway became a triage center. The EMTs raced a gurney down the corridor. Drops of blood fell from the injured man and marred the pristine floor.

I watched with fascination as the doctor and nurses gathered round to assess the situation, all the while continuing to move at a pace close to a run.

One nurse squeezed the IV bag while another shouted out vitals. The doctor yelled above the talking nurse, and somehow it all worked together like a finely choreographed dance.

A hysterical woman raced past me. A small child collapsed to the ground in tears, left behind by a woman whom I assumed was her distraught mother.

I tossed my empty Styrofoam cup in a nearby trashcan and ran toward the child. "Come here, sweetheart." I picked her up and cradled her to my chest. Her breath hiccuped over her cries. "I've got you." The poor thing couldn't be more than three or four. "What's your name?"

She shook in my arms. "Wa…Wa…Weesa." The sorrow in her voice twisted around my heart and squeezed it like a vise.

We made our way to the waiting room where no one had waited for Lisa. It was another reminder of how shit happened when grown-ups lost track of what was important.

I sat down and tried to place her in the seat next to me, but she grabbed my neck like she was in the deep end of the pool, drowning.

"Don't weave me," she cried.

"Never, sweetheart. I'm here." I patted her head and rubbed her back.

It took several minutes of talking and my bag of candy to stop her tears. I read her a magazine article about how to choose lipstick. It was the cleanest thing in the *Cosmo* left behind on the table.

"What's wip dick?" she asked. Her voice still wobbled from the earlier sobs.

In spite of the somber situation, a giggle welled up inside me. "It's lipstick, sweetheart, and it colors your lips." I pressed a finger against her rosy reds. "Try to say it." I broke the word apart. "Say lip."

"Wip," she shouted, her voice echoing through the abandoned hallway.

"Almost." I smiled at her chocolate-covered face. "Now say stick."

"Dick," she yelled.

I looked around, hoping no one heard her. The last thing I needed was to get accused of teaching her bad words.

She practiced until the word *lip* actually came out of her mouth. "Lipdick," she called out around a mouth full of melty chocolate.

"That is a thing, but you're too young to understand." I stood up and hefted her stocky body to my hip. "Let's see if we can find your mommy."

She inhaled a choppy breath, and the tears built in her saucer-like brown eyes. "Daddy got shot."

My insides coiled. "He'll be okay," I assured her, and I wished for her sake I was right.

"Where's your daddy?" she asked.

How did I tell a little one that my father abandoned his family when I was younger than her? That if he hadn't left, my life would be different? "He's on a trip." That wasn't far from the truth. My mom said he packed up his shit and took off after Stacey was born. Two kids were too many.

I walked toward the intake window. As I reached it, a woman came running out of the swinging doors. "Lisa!" she called, her voice full of panic.

"Here she is," I called back. I plopped Lisa onto her sandaled feet and headed for the woman I assumed was her mother.

"Oh, my God. Oh, my God." She pulled the brown-haired girl into her arms, nearly smothering her with kisses. "I'm so sorry." She looked at me. "Thank you."

I looked around the hospital. This was what I wanted to do. I didn't want to marry ketchup bottles or cut pies. I wanted to help people. Today I had.

"You're welcome. I hope you don't mind that I gave her chocolate."

"I'm such a terrible parent."

I wanted to tell her she wasn't, but in truth she was. She'd abandoned her daughter in favor of a man. I had to remind myself that she wasn't my mother, that he was probably the love of her life and not only a guy who warmed her bed.

"It's a good thing I saw her," I said. She'd get no comfort from me.

Comfort belonged to the ones left behind. The ones overlooked. The ones abandoned.

"What do I owe you for the candy?" She reached into her purse and came out with a handful of change.

"You don't owe me anything. You owe her everything." I kneeled before Lisa. "Hey, munchkin, take care of yourself." When I stood, I ruffled her hair and walked back to where Decker had left me.

"You waited." Decker lumbered toward me, looking like he'd aged ten years since he'd gone to see his father. Tufts of his hair poked out in every direction.

"I told you I would." I smoothed his hair with the familiarity of someone who'd known him for a lifetime. "I wouldn't leave you."

He cupped my face, and I thought he might kiss me, but he dropped his head. "I gave you money for cab fare." His voice had that end-of-shift weary tone.

I pulled the bills from my purse and handed them back. He lifted his head. A look of annoyance flashed across his face. "I don't need your money, Decker. I needed to know that you were okay."

He looked at me like he wanted to hug me, and I wished he would.

"You want to get some coffee?" He slung his arm over my shoulder and started for the door.

I pulled him left. "There's a vending machine down the hallway." He tugged me right, and we breezed out the automatic doors.

"I can do better than a vending machine. Besides, I need to get out of here."

We piled into his SUV and drove a few blocks to a twenty-four-hour place that reminded me of where I worked.

We collapsed into a worn booth. It was like time had rewound, and we'd been transported to the '50s. Pictures of Tony Curtis, Elvis, and James Dean covered the wall space. A jukebox sat silently in the corner waiting for a coin. Whereas the diner in Fury was old, this place was authentic.

"Coffee?" the bouffant-wearing waitress asked in a two-pack-a-day voice.

"Coffee for me and…" Decker waited for my order.

"I'll take tea." One way or another, I was getting my tea today.

"You do love tea." He reached for the sugar and the bowl that held the creamers.

"I'm a tea fanatic."

"I'm such an idiot." He rolled his shoulders, causing the tension to lessen one crack at a time. "On our next date, I promise to take you to Dushanbe again…and we'll stay there this time."

"There's going to be a second date?" So much had happened on this date I wasn't sure I could handle a second, although deep inside, I wanted a second, and a third, and a fourth …

"You can't say it hasn't been memorable. Although it's not how I would have liked it to turn out."

Avis the waitress dropped off the drinks and left us alone.

"I don't know. I liked the kiss." My lips tingled at the memory of being in his arms with his mouth against mine.

"It seems like the universe has been against us all day."

After a few dunks of the tea bag into the hot water, the color appeared perfect. "Only today?" Steam rose from the cup and disappeared. "I swear the universe is an evil bitch, and I've been on her radar for life."

He fixed up his coffee so it was white and sweet. "It can't be that bad."

I turned and stared out the window into the night. "It hasn't been good."

Silence surrounded us, and it was nice to be with someone whose presence was enough. To breathe their air and sit in their space was comforting.

Decker was the first to speak. "Before crazy consumed our date, you were going to tell me something."

My heart hitched and stalled for a beat. There was no way I could tell him now. He had enough going on in his life; I didn't need to add to it.

"It was nothing. Tell me about your father."

Chapter 13

DECKER

I ran my hands through my hair. The air left my chest with one forceful gush of wind. Where did I begin? It was half-past ten, and I could talk for hours. "This could take a while." She didn't seem bothered. Nothing but a smile crossed her face.

"It's not like I have another date to make." She relaxed against the window and propped her legs onto the bench. "I'm here for you, Decker."

Avis topped off my coffee and brought another tea for Hannah.

Once the waitress was gone, I began. "For as long as I can remember, I've let my father down." I mirrored Hannah's position, readying myself for the telling of my life story. "I can't remember anything in the early years, but studies show most kids suffer from childhood amnesia. It's a real thing, you know. In general, people can't remember anything from before they were, like, three."

"Are you deflecting again?" She pulled the tea bag out of the steaming water. "We can talk about what Freud called infantile amnesia, or you can tell me why you think your dad is disappointed in you."

"You know about Freud's study?" Every time I was around this girl, she surprised me.

"I told you I wasn't always a waitress. Now move on."

"You're a pushy one, aren't you?" I reached across the table and left my hand palm up. She rested her tiny hand in mine.

"I've learned that you have to ask for what you want and often demand what you need. Right now I need you to tell me why you've decided you're worthless."

"Shall I start a list?" I closed my hand around hers. Something about this girl calmed me. Where everyone else wanted something from me, Hannah wanted nothing but my time and story. One of those things was going to be impossible to give her after tonight.

"No list necessary. I know about the addiction problems, but that comes from something. Usually an unmet need."

"How many psychology classes did you take? You're sounding like a professional. Maybe I should hire you for talk therapy."

"Why hire me if you can have me for free?" Her eyes grew wide. "For talking, I mean." A blush rose up her neck to pink her cheeks.

"Of course that's what you meant." She was beautiful. "But if you weren't, you're undervaluing yourself. You're worth every cent I have."

"Fallen on tough times?"

What was it with this woman? She wanted to point out the value in me, but she didn't see it in herself. "What's with this self-deprecating behavior?"

"It's not so much self-deprecating as self-aware."

I spread my legs and patted the empty space. "Come sit with me." It wasn't a lot of space, but I hoped Hannah would fit.

She came right over. She didn't fit after all, so I pulled her into my lap. Heaven was what it felt like when her head rested against my chest. Her ass pressed to my thighs, and her legs intertwined with mine on the cracked leather seat. She turned her head to me.

She wasn't offering a kiss, but I took it. When my lips touched hers, she surrendered completely. Out of desperation to feel something good, my lips clung to hers. My tongue delved in to taste the sweetness that was her. She half-turned and dug her fingers into my shoulders. She gripped me like I was the stability she needed when in reality, she was the rock for me.

Breathless, we separated.

Avis showed up and slapped our bill on the table. "You kids need to get a room. A kiss like that is wasted in a diner."

I wrapped my arms around Hannah and rested my chin on her shoulder. "A kiss from this girl could never be considered a waste," I said.

Though Avis was older than dirt, there was a light in her eyes that told me she'd been kissed plenty. "You better keep this one, honey. He's easy on the eyes and says the right stuff."

"Oh, he's not my boyfriend. This is therapy."

The old woman's eyes bugged wide. "Where do I sign up for him?"

"My kisses are saved for her," I said, and it felt right. I'd kissed hundreds of girls in my lifetime. Only Hannah's kisses made me feel something soul-deep.

"I'm telling you, young lady, keep this one. At least until he stops saying stuff that makes you swoon."

Hannah loosened my arms and scooted from the seat. "I'm pretty sure he has an entire arsenal of sweet words. He's had a lot of first dates." She grabbed her wallet and pulled out a ten, placing it on top of the four-dollar check. "Keep the change, Avis."

She swiped the ticket and the ten from the table. "You two can come kiss in my station any day." She turned and left us alone.

Hannah stood at the end of my bench and held out her hand. "Let's take a walk, and we can get back to your story."

I scooted to the end and wrapped my arms around her waist for a hug. "Come home with me, and I'll tell you everything."

Hannah laughed. "I said I was free. I never implied I was easy. Besides, I have to work tomorrow."

I stood and towered over her. How could I not? I was six-foot-three, and she was five-foot-nothing. "I wouldn't ask, but I don't want to be alone. A few minutes ago, you told me you learned that you have to ask for what you want and demand what you need. I'm starting with an ask before I move on to a demand. I'm not asking for anything but your presence."

There was a moment of silence where I held my breath and hoped she'd say yes. Not because I wanted to sleep with her—even though I most certainly did—but because I didn't want to be alone with my thoughts or myself.

"It's not nice to throw a girl's words back at her." She tucked her purse under her arm and threaded her fingers through mine. "You better have tea."

"Total screw-up. I could have won your heart with Dushanbe, and I took you to a dive." Before she changed her mind, I raced her to the Rover and helped her in.

When I entered the driver's side, she turned in her seat to face me. "Since we're being honest, I would have loved Dushanbe, but anywhere you are is perfect for me."

Did my heart flop? I'd never been a floppy-hearted kind of guy. Plenty of girls said similar things to me. Why was this one so different? Because she liked *me* and not what I could offer.

"We should pick up your car, but I'm afraid you'll get in it and take off to Fury." Not only was I acting like a total wuss, but I was also telling her my fears. Then again, she was coming to my home for talk therapy, so in a few hours, there would be no place to hide.

"I promise not to run away." She pulled out her phone. "I'm texting my sister in case you decide to eat me." Her hand went straight to her mouth, but it didn't silence her laughter. "Oh, my God, kill me now. That sounded so wrong."

"I don't know. It sounds kind of right to me." My laughter mixed with hers. "Do you always call your sister before someone eats you?"

She reached over and slugged me in the arm. "What I meant was in case you decided to go all Hannibal on me."

"Hannah, when I eat you, and I will, it won't be after I cut you up and cook you for eight hours in a crockpot. I want you raw and wet and wanting." *Holy hell!* That shit came out of nowhere, but I wasn't taking it back. It was the truth.

She squirmed in her seat and then changed the subject. "What's your place like?"

"Now who's deflecting?" Sadly, the drive to Dushanbe was short. As soon as I got her to her car, I knew this conversation would end, and most likely, she'd take off in the opposite direction. "I think we should finish our last conversation, not talk about my place."

"You're right. Let's go back to the beginning. You were talking about your father."

Her phone lit up, giving me another father-free moment. "Does your sister want fingerprints or a hair sample?"

"Of course not." She answered the text. "She wants my thimble collection."

Way too soon, I pulled onto Thirteenth Street. "Which car is yours?"

She lifted up in her seat. "You see that Mercedes?"

I shook my head. She drove a Mercedes? "I see it."

"That's not mine. I'm the light blue piece-of-shit Honda next to it."

I pulled behind her car and parked. "Wow, you're a comedian." It took me seconds to round the Rover and open her door. We walked the few steps to her car. I ribboned my hand through her hair and stole another kiss.

"I am going to follow you. You don't have to drug me with another one of your kisses."

Her hair was so soft between my fingers, her voice was like satin caressing my skin, and she was accusing me of drugging her? I was an addict, for God's sake, and she was my new fix.

"My kisses are all I have to offer." It was all I had that was authentically me.

She lifted onto her toes, which brought the top of her head to my chin. "Don't drive too fast. I know my car looks speedy, but it peaks at fifty-five."

"Hannah, I'll drive ten miles an hour if you stay in my rearview mirror."

She tugged my head down and pressed a quick kiss to my lips. "If you drove seventy, I'd try to keep up."

It was the longest damn thirty-minute drive of my life. Relief washed over me when she pulled right beside me instead of driving past me.

I rushed from the Rover to open her door. Over her shoulder, I looked at my townhouse, trying to see it through her eyes. Too modern? Too pretentious? Too much?

"You live here?" She walked toward the modern brownstone.

"I bought it two years ago." I'd never much cared what people thought of where I lived. I certainly didn't care when my father told me it was a poor investment because I'd never own the land. "It's such a great location. Close to everything."

She eyed it like an artist would the Mona Lisa, taking it all in and forming an opinion without uttering a word.

My hand sat above her perfect ass, right at the dip in the small of her back that fit my palm perfectly. "My place is over here." We walked to the end unit, I pressed my thumb to the scanner, and the door popped open.

"Pretty fancy." Her shoes clicked on the black granite floor, and she looked up to the glass ceiling that sat three stories above. "How big is this place?"

Automatic lights turned on as we walked through the hallway. "It's over three thousand square feet. Not huge by any stretch, but too big for me by myself." Fourteen steps took us to the second floor. "The first floor has a home gym, an office, and a bathroom." The kitchen lights flickered to life. "This floor has two bedrooms, a kitchen, living room, and two bathrooms."

Her eyes went to the next flight of stairs up. "What's up there?"

I opened the cupboard and grabbed two mugs. "There are two bedrooms, two bathrooms, and a rooftop deck." I filled the cups with water and microwaved them to a near boil.

"You have a rooftop deck?" She slid the stool away from the center island and climbed onto the seat.

The pantry was stocked with several teas because I'd read once that it was good for you. It also helped me sleep. "I've got Sleepytime, Lemon Lift, Moroccan Mint from Dushanbe, and English breakfast, which is fine to drink all day long if you ask me."

Her giggle floated through the air like a song. "Unless, of course, you plan to sleep, then it's not recommended. I made it through three years of finals on English breakfast tea."

I set the tea boxes in front of her. She picked Moroccan Mint. Hannah would have loved Dushanbe. I'd have to make that blunder up to her.

KELLY COLLINS

"I hate that you didn't get to finish college." I scooped loose tea into the metal strainer and dunked it into the hot water. "Will you go back?"

"Someday, I hope."

I dipped a Sleepytime tea bag into my cup. Once hers had steeped the recommended time, I took her upstairs to the rooftop deck.

"It's peaceful up here." With the flick of a switch, the fire pit flamed to life. "This is my favorite place besides The Dive." She took a seat in front of the glass barrier, and I plopped comfortably beside her. We sipped our tea silently until I gained the strength to tell her everything.

Chapter 14

HANNAH

My hand automatically rested on his thigh as a gesture of comfort and safety. Whatever he wanted to share would stay with me. If I could keep Ryker's and Silas's secret, then I wouldn't betray Decker either.

"About my father…" He sipped at his tea. "He's a hard man who can't be pleased. Especially by me."

I stayed silent so he would continue. He talked about never belonging. Never being able to gain his father's favor. "It's like I'm not even his son. He treats me like someone dumped me on his doorstep, and he felt some obligation to feed and clothe me."

I had no idea how Decker came to be in the household of the Rileys, but he wasn't far off from the truth.

I spread my arms open in front of me. "A man who didn't love you wouldn't give you all this."

He sat for a minute in silence. "I earned this. I've worked selling homes since I could talk. The only good thing about my dad is that he always pays me my commissions."

"So you're good at what you do. That's wonderful. You should focus on that."

He stared into the fire pit. "Are you a good waitress?"

I knew where he was going. "Most days."

"Do you love it?"

"No, it's something I have to do."

"Exactly. I sell real estate because I have to, and now I have to devote my life to it because it's what my dad expects. How can I disappoint him when he's dying?"

Decker and I seemed like polar opposites. He lived in a fancy townhouse and drove a pricey car; I lived in an old beat-up bungalow on Happy Drive and drove a ten-year-old heap of metal on worn tires. But somehow we had compatible souls.

He picked me up and sat me on his lap. When he played with my hair, it sent shivers all the way down my spine to my girly bits. It would be so easy to ask him to take me to bed—to make love to me. It might even be the best night of my life.

"It's exhausting being everything to everyone. How do you cope?"

"I used to drink vodka. Now I drink tea and drive motorcycles too fast."

"Both vices haven't worked well for you."

"I don't know, I met you, and it seems to be going okay. How do you cope?"

I snuggled in closer to his body heat and set my hand on his broad chest. His heart beat steadily under my palm. "There are days when people tax my nerves, and sometimes I accidentally trip while delivering their food." I lifted my shoulders in a shrug. "It happens."

He laughed. "Remind me to never agitate you."

"Too late. You've been agitating me since I met you, but in a good way."

"And I'm not wearing food yet."

"Give it time. I'm sure you'll do something trip-worthy. The key is to order something that won't soak into your clothes. Chocolate shakes are the worst."

"I'll stick to grilled cheese and water."

"You're a smart man."

His body shook with his laugh. "If I were smart, I would have taken you someplace other than The Dive." His hands wrapped around my waist. My head settled on his shoulder.

"I love that you are sharing your story with me. I'm here for you."

"Why?"

"Because somewhere inside of me, I know you're worth it." It was one of those moments where my heart clenched in agreement. It was rare that my head and heart agreed.

"Something tells me that's a huge compliment." He turned his head and kissed me. Not a sweet brush-of-the-lips kiss, but a torn-from-the-heart, passionate kiss. One that made my insides burn with desire.

Our lips separated when I leaned back. I focused on drawing air into my lungs as the aftermath of his kiss coursed through my body. I thought about his confessions and knew I owed him some of mine.

"You need to know something about me."

He nibbled up my jawline to my ear. "Tell me everything." His hand moved to my waist, then up my dress to cup my breast. I had ample material to work with, but his hand completely covered my boob. I pressed my hand over his and stopped the movement because with his hands on me, I couldn't think.

"I want to have sex with you, but you need to know I'm not the kind of girl who goes to bed with every guy on the first date." Unfortunately, my being blonde, big-boobed, and built for sex gave men the wrong idea about me.

"This is like our second date. We had coffee and pie the first time." He ran his tongue down my neck, making gooseflesh rise on my skin.

I squirmed in his lap, trying to stop the tingling desire that flooded my system. "Seriously, you need to know that I'm not some easy girl." I pushed him back. His blue eyes were heavy with desire. "Lots of men think I am, but I'm not. Two men have tried to rape me."

He jolted back. "Oh, my God. I'm so sorry." He pushed me gently from his lap to sit at his side. The absence of his touch was worse than the sting of my truth. "I don't want you to think I brought you here for sex."

Feeling bold, I climbed back onto his lap and wrapped my arms around his neck. "You're not understanding," I said. "Those men tried to take something from me that I wasn't willing to give. But you…" I pressed my lips to his for a brief second. "I want to give you everything." I'd had a few partners. Not as many as everyone would guess. I was a flirt, not a whore. But my desire to be with Decker was stronger than anything I'd felt. I was willing to risk everything for one night—tonight.

"I'd never hurt you, Hannah."

I shifted to straddle his legs so I could see his face fully. "I believe that you wouldn't hurt me intentionally. Now kiss me so this moment can wash away the stress from the day."

His hand tightened in my hair, and his mouth took possession of my lips. He drove me mad with his hungry kisses. Our tongues tangled in a battle that sent pleasure soaring from my nipples to my sex.

When I was sure my lips were bruised, I broke the kiss. I crawled off his lap and pulled him to a standing position. "Where's your room?"

Those heavy-lidded eyes brightened for the first time in hours. Decker needed a drug tonight. I knew that was why he needed me to be here with him. I was his temporary vice to get through the night. My only hope was that I was as enticing and intoxicating as a bottle of vodka or a line of cocaine.

"Are you sure? I didn't invite you—"

"That's what makes it sweeter. This is on my terms. Not yours. Are you sure you want me?" I walked backward, unfastening the tiny pearl-like buttons on the front of my dress.

"Oh, Hannah, what have you done to me?"

"Oh, Decker, I haven't done anything to you yet, but I have plans."

One long step and he was in front of me. One lift and I was in his arms. One short walk down the hallway and we were in his room, where he tumbled me onto his bed. A lamp on the nightstand cast a soft glow across the room. Like the rest of his house, it was modern with simple lines and monochromatic colors. The bedspread was soft below me. His body was hard above me, especially the stiff rod that prodded my thigh.

He tugged at my buttons while I pulled at his shirt.

"Let me," we said in unison and laughed. He rolled off me and onto his feet. Propped up on my elbows I watched him undress. The surrounding air arced with energy, a strong current pinging between us.

When his shirt cleared his chest, I took a deep fortifying breath. The way he moved his tall lean body set my pulse pounding. He was like a fever in my blood, the heat raging through my veins and settling in my core.

One at a time, he pulled off my heels and tossed them to the floor. With a swift pull of my ankles, he slid my body to the edge of the bed. Gathering up the hem of my dress, he shimmied it past my hips and removed it completely. Left in my pink panties and bra, I should have felt naked because I nearly was. But all I felt was beautiful in his eyes.

The hunger written on his face was enough to prove he desired me, and I was as ravenous for him.

"You're so damn beautiful." He dropped to his knees in front of me. I'd never brought a man to his knees before, and the feeling was heady and wonderful. "I want to see every inch of you." One strap lowered at a time, he exposed my breasts. My nipples puckered under his gaze. He pulled one into his mouth and savored it. Not the way some men suck it in like boba stuck in a straw, but like he was enjoying my taste and texture all at once.

While I reached back to free my bra, his hands tugged at my panties. He tugged them down to my ankles, and I kicked them off, not knowing or caring where they landed.

"I need to taste your sweetness." His hands gripped my knees and pulled my legs apart. My eyes closed as I tried to control the trembling. The heat of his tongue licked through my sex, sending desire jolting through my body.

A low groan left my lips when his tongue pressed inside me. He circled my bundle of nerves, forcing my hips to rise and seek more. He grabbed my ass and pulled me closer to his mouth, intensifying my desire.

"Damn, that feels so good." Weeks ago I was swearing off men forever, and now I was swearing because this man felt so perfect between my thighs. He licked at me with long deliberate strokes.

Whimpers and incoherent sounds left my mouth. My fingers gripped his hair. The velvet of his tongue dipped inside me. "Decker!" I cried out. It swirled around me while his lips pulled in the engorged button for a suck. My breath grew rapid and jagged. My body shook. His fingers slid into my wetness and I came hard in body-racking spasms.

He slowed his strokes but never stopped. His fingers slid in and out of me while the last of my spasms gripped them. When the final shudder left me, Decker pulled back and wiped his glistening lips with the back of his hand.

He smiled with the kind of pride you see when a football player wins the Super Bowl. Still dressed in jeans, he climbed up my body and kissed me, my taste on his lips more arousing than gross.

"Hannah." His voice was sex drugged. "You're my new favorite meal."

My hands splayed over his chest. My fingertips memorized each muscle, each dip, and divot that made him so perfect. I explored his exposed body from the top of his head to his buttoned jeans. Braced above my body, his arms bulged. The muscles pulled at the gauze stretching across his wound.

"Does it hurt still?" My fingertips brushed lightly over the area.

"No." Transferring his weight to his knees, he took my hand and pressed it to his rock-hard erection. "This hurts."

One tug and a swift zip down gave me access to the fullness of him. The man was big everywhere. "Take off your pants."

His smile was disarming, and if I weren't already naked, the heat in his eyes would have incinerated my clothes.

Not only was he hot, he was fast. Naked in seconds flat, he climbed up my body and let his heavy length fall between my legs. "I've thought about this with you so many times since that first night. It's a wonder I've accomplished anything."

"I'm already naked with my legs spread. You don't have to sweet-talk me." It was heaven to feel the heat radiate off his body. To watch his eyes eat me up inch by inch. His words made me wish for more, but that was dangerous. Girls like me didn't get to wish. We accepted what was right here, right now.

"Hannah, I want to punch every man who's never told you how incredible you are."

Maybe I could wish just tonight. "I don't need to hear it from any man but you." His torso lengthened as he reached for his nightstand. When he relaxed over me, he held a condom in his hand. The package read *magnum*, and I didn't doubt it for a second.

I watched with fascination as he rolled the tiny piece of latex over what could only be described as massive. There was no doubt that tomorrow I'd still feel him.

Decker looked into my eyes like he was diving into my soul. "I don't deserve you, Hannah, but I want you so bad." He probed at my sex but didn't push forward. "You are special."

The same care he took with his tongue he took with the rest. He didn't shove forward and seize his pleasure. He inched in, building mine. *Full* didn't describe my body when he was deep inside—only the word *complete* could.

My hands cupped his granite-hard ass and pulled him deeper. My hips rotated beneath his thrusting body. "Hannah, you're going to make me come."

"That is the end game, right?" He'd given me pleasure like I'd never known. I wanted him to experience the same.

He pulled out almost completely. "Yes, but for both of us." His strokes began again. They started at a slow pace and built into a deep thrusting rhythm that set my nerve endings aflame.

He pushed one of my legs back, and the position changed everything. Every thrust was a direct connection to that bundle of nerves that was ready to spark and explode.

I was close. He was close. I clawed at his back. "Hannah, you are so freaking right for me." I'd been on the edge, and his words took me over. I tumbled hard and fast.

My core pulsed around him, and he grew impossibly bigger before he stilled and my name burst from his lips. Never had a man called my name when he came. I'd heard things like "Damn, girl" to indiscernible grunts, but this man called my name, and it was the most amazing sound ever.

His weight pushed me into the mattress, but it wasn't uncomfortable at all. In fact, it was comforting. His body was a shield on top of me. Seconds later he shifted to the side and brushed his lips over mine.

"Thank you for being with me."

This was the awkward moment where I wasn't sure whether I should climb out of bed and get dressed or snuggle up close to his body and drift off to sleep. I attempted to roll away, but he pulled me close. "Stay with me."

Not wanting to sound too eager, I said, "I have to work at nine."

"I'll make sure you're up. I'll even make pancakes and tea." He rolled out of bed and walked his fine ass to the bathroom. He peeked his head out of the door. "I have a spare toothbrush, and I'll get you a T-shirt, although I prefer you naked."

"Sold." I rose from the bed and wrapped his comforter around my body. "I need to get my phone to check on my mom."

He strutted out of the bathroom, smelling like mint. After rummaging through his drawer, he pulled out a blue T-shirt and tossed it to me. "I'll get your phone. You get ready for bed."

When I walked into the bathroom, things were ready for me. A new toothbrush. A tube of paste. A clean washcloth and a towel. They were simple niceties that no one had ever thought to give me.

Face scrubbed and teeth brushed, I walked back into the bedroom to find him under the covers with the blankets thrown back for me. My purse sat on my side of the bed.

I sent off a quick message to Stacey telling her I was staying with a friend and to look after Mom. I tucked myself up close to Decker's body and relaxed.

"Best night of my life." He kissed the back of my head and pulled me to his body.

"Mine too." After a day of work and a night of romance—plus the fact that it was past two in the morning—I was slipping into that twilight rest, that place where your body is asleep but your mind is still functioning.

Decker shifted. His hand rested on my naked hip. Words that were a whisper fell from his lips. "I found you when I needed you. You are perfect for me."

I stayed still, not wanting to interrupt him. His soft words soothed my once wounded heart. His words stitched me back together. He wanted me. He needed me. I was perfect for him.

His breath tickled my neck.

"Right person. Wrong time. How will I tell you I can't have you?"

It took everything in me to stay still. My heart was warmed and pliable from Decker's kind words, ripe and ready for the picking. But he didn't gently pluck it; he reached in and yanked it out, then stomped on it.

Despite my exhaustion, I stayed awake until I was sure he was sound asleep. That's when I slipped from his bed, gathered my things, and left brokenhearted.

MY ASS DRAGGED through my shift. The old owl clock seemed to lose its hoot as the hands moved slowly around the face.

I'd "accidentally" spilled several plates on customers. Making anyone who looked at me wrong pay for Decker's sins.

Deep down inside, I knew he liked me, but it didn't take the sting of his words away. He knew he was going to walk away, and yet he took what I offered anyway.

I wavered between hating myself and hating him, and in the end, I couldn't hate either of us. I'd wanted him, and I'd offered myself to him. My exact thoughts had been that I'd take him, if only for one night, and I got exactly what I'd asked for: one night.

The bell rang. The door opened. The Savages walked in.

"You look like shit." Ryker folded his big body into the booth and reached for the sugar and creamer. "That date either went really good or really bad."

"It was fine."

Silas leaned back. "Uh oh, bro. You know when a girl says, 'It was fine,' that means it was anything but fine."

I poured their coffees. "You don't know anything."

Silas sipped his black coffee while Ryker turned his white and sweet.

"I know that you look like you were ridden hard and put away wet," Ryker said. He tapped Silas's mug. "Looks like our baby brother's got game."

"You're such an asshole. I don't know what I ever saw in you. For your information, Decker's dad has cancer, and we were at the hospital."

"Oh, shit. That's bad. Is Decker okay?" Silas asked, all humor gone from his voice.

I had to give the brothers some credit. They'd looked for so long and were finally rewarded, yet they were trying to proceed with caution and concern and tenderness.

"He's handling it." There was no way I was going to tell them that I helped get him through the night by screwing the sorrow out of him. "Are you going to order something?"

They both nodded, and I made an attempt to walk away, but Ryker reached out and gently grabbed my wrist.

"I'm sorry. I was an asshole." The blue eyes that once looked at me with irritation now looked at me with remorse.

My gaze flickered between the two brothers. "Seems to be a Savage trait."

"Was the date that bad?" Silas scooted over and patted the seat next to him. "Sit down and tell us about it."

No convincing was needed to get me to plop my ass down. "No, he's a nice guy. He's not for me." Those words ripped at my insides. That seemed to be the way of it when I lied. My mouth let the lie flow forth, but my gut always had a visceral reaction like an internal lie detector.

"Is he happy?" Ryker asked.

I braced myself for more stomach pain but instead avoided it with the truth. "He's well off, sure of who he is, and where he needs to be." No lie there, only the omission of the complete truth.

"That's that, I guess," Silas said.

Both men seemed to wilt in their seats.

"You should stay in touch with him. His father is dying, and he might need some support." In front of my eyes, they bloomed. "He'll need friends."

Chapter 15

DECKER

Ever since I'd woken up yesterday and found Hannah gone, living had felt like walking through hell. No note...nothing. She wouldn't answer my texts. Didn't answer my calls.

I stared out the window of Dad's office at nothing and everything. Riley Realty sat in a prime location downtown. Situated on the top floor, the views were magnificent, but all of a sudden seemed lackluster.

Rose, Dad's secretary, poked her head in. "Mr. Riley?"

It was funny to be called by Dad's name. I turned around, expecting him to be behind me looking over my work. Evaluating and criticizing every dotted *i* and crossed *t*. Oh, he was there all right, but not in the flesh. He lived in my head, constantly reminding me that I wasn't enough.

"Rose, you've known me since I was born. Call me Decker... please. Mr. Riley will always be my father, and I am not my father."

The older woman nodded. In her early fifties, she looked much older, but I imagine that came with the job. "Your mother is here."

I rolled my lower lip between two fingers. If Mom was here, that meant Dad was doing better. Maybe he'd surprise us and make it out of the hospital after all.

"Send her in."

Dressed in navy blue and white Chanel, Mom looked like she'd walked hot off a magazine cover, not out of the hospital ICU.

I stood up and gave her a kiss on the cheek. "You can walk in, Mom. You never need an invitation or an announcement."

"I brought tea." In her hands were two cardboard to-go cups. There was no doubt she'd stopped by Dushanbe. "Moroccan Mint for you. Oolong for me."

Normally, I'd be pleased with her selfless gesture, but even the smell made my chest tighten. Somehow I'd messed it up with Hannah. I couldn't get the woman out of my mind, and as evidenced by her complete dismissal, I was obviously purged from her thoughts.

"John tells me you were on a date when we brought your father to the hospital." Mom placed her tea on the desk and sat in the chair in front. "He says she's a nice girl. Tell me about her. Hannah, is it?" She smoothed her skirt with her hands, and then gave me that mom look that said, *tell me everything.*

"We had one date, and that was it. She's not interested." A punch to the chest would have felt better than admitting that.

"What happened?" Always poised, Mom should have been the first lady of the United States, not the first lady of an egotistical real estate mogul.

"It's not a good time, Mom." I twirled my finger in the air. "Look around you. Do I seem like the kind of guy who's going to have time to date?"

Mom was like a professional poker player. Her face rarely showed her emotions. Her only give was a slight nibble of her lower lip.

"Decker, I'm proud of you, but this is your dad's legacy. Not yours." She leaned across the table and took my hands. "If you like this girl, make time for her."

"I liked her plenty, but it's too complicated."

Mom's thumbs rubbed across my knuckles. "Your dad was always driven. It was one of the things I fell in love with. He pursued me as hard as he did the next sale. Don't think for a minute he didn't go after what he wanted with vigor."

It only made me feel worse to hear Dad took the time to get

what he wanted because I never felt like he'd taken the time for me. Then again, he did spend countless hours teaching me the business—involving me in and entrusting me with his most prized possession. Maybe every red mark on a contract, every look of disapproval was his way of telling me he loved me. Life was too damn confusing.

"It is my legacy. It's what he wants, and I'll be damned if I'll disappoint him."

"I love that you want to please him. But at the end of the day, it's more important that you make yourself happy. Your father lived by his own set of rules. You should too."

I rubbed the exhaustion from my eyes. I had dove into my new normal. Meetings were intense. Work was hard. Time evaporated quickly. "How is Dad?" I stopped by the hospital yesterday once I'd delivered the contract to the bank. Instead of an *atta boy*, I got a long list of new to-dos.

Mom's eyes filled with sorrow. "When he's not in pain, he's a tyrant. When he is in pain, he's worse. They've given him a morphine button."

I struggled to come to terms with this love/hate thing I had going with my father. I didn't want him to die and me to be left with regret. That thought alone reinforced the decision I made, in that moment, to be everything he wanted me to be.

"I'll stop by the hospital later."

She leaned back and picked up her tea. "He'll love that. He lights up when you come to visit."

Yeah, but it's not happiness, it's the flames of agitation and anger that make him glow. "Can I bring anything?"

"No, sweetheart, we have everything we need." Mom took her tea and left. I stared at mine and thought about Hannah. Clearly, it had all been too much for a first date.

———

THE SUN HAD SET when I walked into the hospital with a briefcase full of contracts—signed contracts. I'd busted my ass all day to get ahead of the game. Poor Rose looked pale with exhaustion when she left.

I marched into Dad's room with a confidence that only existed on the surface. At some point in the day, I'd decided the only way to deal with my father was to go in with a take-no-prisoners attitude.

"Hey, Dad." I ignored his orange skin and haunting yellow eyes. I pulled up a chair on the other side of the bed across from where my mother sat.

"Decker? Shouldn't you be at work?"

"I was at work for twelve hours." I set the briefcase on the edge of the bed. "I wanted to bring the contracts I've worked out today. We have five closings tomorrow. Three on Wednesday. Thursday I'm booked with meetings. Friday I go into final negotiations for the Trident Building." I pulled out a stack of folders and set them on his chest. "I wanted you to know that things are going fine. I've got it under control." I wouldn't tell him that each contract I read made me want to rush to the nearest bar and drink a bottle. That each meeting made my insides churn like a hundred hornets were buzzing and stinging me at random.

"You did all that?" Dad tried to sit up but was too weak. Mom pressed the button that brought him upright.

"It's what you pay me to do." I closed the briefcase. "I've got to go. I'm meeting a friend."

"Hannah?" Mom asked.

"Not tonight." I offered Dad a handshake. His once firm grip was frail and weak. "Happy reading."

After a quick kiss and hug for Mom, I left. My first stop was the liquor store for a bottle of vodka. My second stop was The Dive so I could give Tanner a chance to talk me out of plunging into hell.

Like usual he was manning the bar.

"You look like hell, man." Tanner's eyes missed nothing, especially the bag-covered bottle in my left hand. "You on the fence? Or have you fallen off already?"

I slammed the unopened bottle on the bar. "Still sealed but calling to me. No, that's not accurate. It's screaming my damn name so loud I can't think of anything else." *Except Hannah.*

"This about your dad?"

"I'm not sure anymore. It's about a lot of things."

Tanner took the bottle, opened the top and poured the liquid down the sink. "Start talking."

I'd done the same thing for him when his wife left him. She was also an alcoholic and didn't like him sober. He didn't like her drunk. Also a fixer, Tanner tried to lure her to the light side—the sober side. But she preferred the dark.

I told him about working my ass off and hating every minute of it. "I'm not lazy," I stated. "I'm all in when it's a good cause. I don't see world domination by land deals a worthy use of my time or resources."

"What do you want to do?" He poured me a cup of coffee and leaned against the back bar.

"I want to be a fixer like you and Hannah. I want to end my life knowing I made someone's life better."

"You're doing that now with your dad." He said it with a shrug. "Finish what you started. It doesn't have to be a lifetime choice. Just a choice that doesn't leave you with regrets."

He was right. The only thing was, it felt like a lifetime decision. "He wants me to grow old and gray behind that desk."

Tanner wiped at the already clean counter. "And JC Penney started as a catalog. Everything changes. If you continue to live in the past, you'll never have a future. Now tell me about Hannah. She's a cute thing."

I gave him the abbreviated version. I left out the hot sex and went straight to her refusal to take my calls.

"Is she a worthy cause?" Tanner grinned at me. I knew that look. It said, *I'm giving a lesson with your words.*

"She could be everything." Even before I'd tasted her and had sunk myself deep inside her, she had been in me. She'd burrowed under my skin with her smile and her laughter. I liked the spunky side of her that threatened me with a butter knife before she bandaged my arm.

"Then I imagine you should go all in."

My fingers ran over the rough scabbed skin destined to become a scar, but it would be one I'd remember fondly because it had brought me to Hannah.

"You're right. She ran, and I need to know why." I tossed a twenty on the bar.

"You know you don't have to pay for anything here." He pushed the twenty toward me.

"Keep it, man. You saved me again. Surely that's worth twenty bucks."

Tanner chuckled. "Tonight I'll go to sleep knowing I did something worthwhile."

Chapter 16

HANNAH

Decker had stopped calling and texting two days ago. I should have been relieved, but my heart felt heavy. It was like some curse had rolled through town and now hovered endlessly over the Banning house.

"Mom," I called. "You've got ten minutes."

She'd been mostly sober for a week. But last night, I'd caught her sneaking a whiskey bottle out of the toilet tank. That had been the action to push me over the tipping point. I poured it down the drain and made her some tea. "It was a little to take the edge off," she whined. I coaxed her into the kitchen and talked with her into the middle of the night. I informed her I was taking her to meet someone. I hoped Tanner was willing to speak to my mother. More importantly, I hoped he would help her. Decker talked about him like he was a savior. And that was something I needed. I was worn thin.

Miracle of miracles, she walked into the kitchen looking more like her old self. "Does this place have good food?"

"You're hungry?" That was good. Mom had lost interest in almost everything besides drugs and alcohol, including food. For years, she'd been drinking her calories instead of eating them. "They have the best green chili burger known to man."

I rushed her out the door and into my car before she changed her mind.

"NOW YOU'RE TALKING," Mom said when we walked into The Dive. I wasn't sure whether it was because the food smelled great or because she thought it was a bar.

"There's no booze here, Mom."

She gave me a *duh* look and then lifted her nose into the air. "I can smell the chili." At least that part of her anatomy wasn't turned to off.

I looked over to the table where Decker and I had sat. It was empty, but it didn't seem right to sit there. That was our special place. Hell, I wouldn't have come back to this place if it weren't for Mom. She needed help I couldn't give her, and I prayed Tanner could guide her in a better direction.

"Hannah," Tanner called out. "What brings you here?"

"Couldn't resist the Dexner special." I led Mom to an open table on the other side of the bar.

"Glad you're here." He looked toward Mom. "And who's this beauty next to you?"

Mom's smile warmed her tired sallow complexion. "I'm Rachel. Hannah's mother."

Did I see a spark flash in her eyes, or was that me being hopeful?

"Well, Rachel, Hannah's mother, it's lovely to meet you. Do you trust me?"

My heart flipped in my stomach. Decker had said the same thing to me on our first date.

"I trust no one." Mom's lips pulled into a thin line.

"Smart woman. However, I'm only asking because Hannah mentioned the Dexner."

Mom's tight expression softened. "Are you a good cook?"

Tanner shook his head. "Hell no. That task I leave to the professionals."

"Smart man," my mom volleyed back. "I'll trust you until you give me a reason to doubt you."

Tanner turned to me. "Decker was here last night. He mentioned you."

Talk about a punch to the chest. "Really?" I wanted to ask a thousand questions, but for what purpose? The man had already told me he couldn't pursue anything with me. "I hope he's well." I busied myself with unwrapping the silverware.

"He'd be better if you answered his calls."

Before I could reply, Tanner turned and walked away.

"Who's Decker?" Mom asked.

"He's no one." The pain of the lie nearly doubled me over. I hated the betrayal that stabbed deep in my gut, but it held me to a level of honesty within myself despite the lies that came from my lips.

"Sounds like someone to me." Mom pulled the napkin I'd been shredding from my hand and let it fall to the pile of torn pieces. "Talk to me."

Instead of looking at her, I glanced at the pile of shredded paper and went to work puzzling them back together.

"I didn't bring you here to talk about me. I brought you here to meet Tanner. He's Decker's AA sponsor, and I thought…" What *did* I think? I hadn't even asked Tanner whether he was willing to talk to my mom. Was it fair of me to bulldoze them both into a plan?

"That guy is an alcoholic?" Mom shook her head. "But he's so handsome and put together."

"Yes, but he's in recovery. He doesn't drink anymore. He helps those who do."

"And this Decker is an alcoholic?" Mom crossed her arms and frowned the way she used to when I was in trouble. "I don't want you hanging out with alkies and druggies."

The hypocrisy of her statement made me laugh. Not a funny giggle, but a hysterical kind of cackle. "If that's true, you need to say goodbye to me and be on your way." Is this what they called tough love?

"I'm your mother." Her words came out in a coarse staccato that marched up my spine to the base of my skull where the logical part of my brain took over.

"Yes, you are, but when are you going to start acting like it?"

Mom sat there with her mouth open but no words spewing forth.

"You checked out years ago," I said.

She buried her face in her hands. Muffled words escaped between her fingers. "I failed you that day. I ruined everything we had."

Rage that had been building for years burst forth like a flare. "*He* ruined everything we had. You didn't begin to fail me until you turned from your kids to the bottle." I should have said *bottles*, but it didn't matter whether it was a bottle of booze or a bottle of pills. The fact was, Mom had numbed her pain by numbing herself.

Tears mixed with mascara ran down her face. "I had nothing to offer you."

"You're a piece of work." I wanted to get up and walk out. "I'm tired of people abandoning me. Get your shit together, or get out of my life. I don't have time for people who aren't committed."

Tanner walked up with two Dexner specials and two sodas. He stumbled back when I tossed what I'd made yesterday on the table and stood. The pile of crumpled ones would have to be enough to pay for lunch and a cab for Mom.

"Tanner, it was great to see you. Can you call a cab for my mom when she's finished?"

His slight nod gave me permission to hightail it out of the restaurant.

When I got home, Stacey was sitting on the couch with Mark. "What the hell is he doing here?"

They both ignored me and went back to watching TV.

I stomped into the kitchen to make some tea. While it steeped, the phone rang, and I had every intention of ignoring it until I saw the caller ID—University of Boulder.

"Hello," I answered too curtly.

A deep resonating voice spoke. "This is Cade Matthews from admissions. I'm calling for Stacey Banning."

"Hold on, please." I walked to the doorway between the kitchen and the living room, but Stacey and Mark weren't there. "Stacey," I called out. All I heard was giggling coming from the bedroom. I wanted to shake some sense into my sister.

"I'm sorry, she's unavailable. Can I take a message?"

"Can you tell her that her withdrawal has been processed, and she has a credit of three hundred and fifty-one dollars? We'll send a check."

"What do you mean, 'her withdrawal has been processed'?"

After a pause, the man said, "She dropped out of school."

I slammed the phone down and marched straight to her room. The door opened so hard it swung back and hit me in the head, but that didn't sting as much as seeing Mark's naked ass moving as he pumped inside of my baby sister. My eyes burned from the sight. I'd never un-see that shit.

"Get the hell out." My voice was straight out of *Poltergeist*.

Mark hopped off the bed with his junk bobbing.

I looked at his unwrapped willy. "Really, Stacey? No condom?"

"That's none of your business!" Stacey screamed. She climbed off the bed and put her hand on his shoulder. "You can't kick him out. This is my house too."

My body shook with rage at the two naked people standing in front of me. "When you pay the damn rent, you can make the rules." I tossed my sister's discarded dress at her. "Get some clothes on." Mark was quickly going limp. "You too, asshole. I don't want to look at your tiny willy anymore." Compared to Decker, Mark's thing was a child's toy. "In the kitchen now." I stormed out of her room, slamming the door behind me.

Back in the kitchen, I sipped the cup of calming chamomile tea I'd made before the fateful phone call and waited. The front door shut, and a motorcycle engine growled to life. Minutes later Stacey stood in front of me.

"What the hell is your problem?" she yelled.

"You quit school?" I hung on to the last straw of calm I had in me. Nothing would come out of this conversation if we both continued to yell.

"I hated school. I wasn't doing it for me. I did it because you made me."

"Do you want to be a waitress?" I blurted. "Do you want to waste your entire life doing something you don't want to do?"

"No, that's why I quit school. I don't want to be a teacher. I want to be a mother."

"I didn't give up my life so you could get knocked up by Mark the asshole."

"I didn't ask you to do that! I didn't ask you to be unhappy for me!"

"Don't you get it?" I walked to the table and pulled out a chair for her. She looked at it and stood her ground. "He's not going to make you happy!"

"What do you know? You can't even get a man." The truth of her words stung like a paper cut dipped in rubbing alcohol.

"I can get a man. The difference between you and me is, I won't settle for any man. I won't accept being second fiddle to a motorcycle club or a night out with the boys or another woman. I want a man who doesn't think that hopping on his bike and taking off for two years is okay."

"Good luck with that. Never forget you live in Fury."

The growl of the engine seeped into the house. "Mark's waiting for me." She started for the door.

"You should expect more for yourself," I said.

She turned around and smiled. "Get used to him, Hannah, he's the father of my unborn child." Stacey's hand went to her flat belly.

My hands clutched my stomach. All I wanted to do was throw up.

I went to my room and fell onto my bed. Curled into the fetal position, I cried until my eyes drooped and nothingness took over.

Eventually, voices came from the kitchen. I dragged my groggy ass out of bed and went to see who was talking. To my surprise, Mom sat with Tanner at the scarred kitchen table.

Both of them looked up at me.

"Good evening, Hannah."

I acknowledged him with a single word. "Tanner."

He stood. "I should let you go, but I'll be here at eight in the morning to pick you up. You need to be clean and sober, or it won't work." Tanner walked past me and out the door.

I sat down in the chair he vacated. "What was that all about?"

"I've got a job and a sponsor."

WASN'T it funny how life gave and took? In one day, I'd lost my sister and gotten my mom back. Stacey hadn't come home last night, but Mom did, and she hadn't been fully present for a long time.

I topped off old man Tucker's coffee cup. "Anything else, Bob?"

His double chin wobbled when he smiled. "If you're granting wishes, I'd like to be forty years younger and on a date with you, young lady."

I bent over and kissed his bald head. "It's always good to dream, Bob." I made my rounds and went back to the counter to cut pie. I no longer jumped a foot in the air when the bell above the door rang. Decker had eased me past the fear that all men were there to hurt me, sort of. I still believed it was true, but now I knew that not all men used their fists; some used their words. I wasn't sure which was more painful. The bruises on the skin faded, but the scars inside seemed to hurt a lot longer.

A man with a package stood at the counter. "Are you Hannah?"

I put down the knife. "That's me."

"This is for you." He pulled a card out of his pocket and set it on top of the box. "The person who sent it suggested you read the card first." He waited for a tip before he turned and walked away.

Only one person had ever sent me anything, and that was Decker. There was no doubt in my mind this was from him.

My hands shook. I slid my finger under the flap of the envelope and opened it. It was stationery with his name on it—Decker Owen Riley. Was it crazy that I brushed across the letters like I was touching him? I opened the card slowly and took in the gracefulness of his writing. Elongated and loopy, it popped off the page and into my heart.

Hannah,

You are worth far more than I gave. The last days have been unbearable without a word from you. I don't know where I messed up. All I know is I'm desperate for another chance. I'll be waiting when you get off work tonight.

Decker

He'll be waiting? My hands went straight to my face. No makeup, no mascara, no lip-gloss. Hell, I almost hadn't brushed my hair. In the end, I pulled it into a high ponytail and called it good. I was a mess on both the inside and outside.

I looked around, making sure no one was watching. For some reason, this gift seemed special. I eased the top off and found a beautiful teapot, two matching cups, and the biggest bag of Moroccan Mint tea I'd ever seen. Everything was labeled from Dushanbe. A tiny handwritten note sat on top.

It's not enough, but it's a start.

D

The damn man didn't bring me to Dushanbe. He brought Dushanbe to me. Flowers decorated the pot. The forget-me-nots were no accidental purchase. He chose the teapot with care and consideration. I opened the bag of tea and inhaled the rich mint scent. I wanted to stay angry with Decker, but it was impossible. Maybe I'd been wrong to judge him. Maybe I should have stayed for pancakes, tea, and an explanation.

The owl clock ticked away faster than I could imagine. I shuffled Ana, Grace, and Mona out of the diner with haste in hopes that I could hang the closed sign five minutes early and put myself together, but I had no such luck: Decker walked in as my guardian angels walked out. They stopped a second to stare before they climbed into Ana's Jeep and left.

"You're early." I fiddled with my hair.

Decker looked around the empty restaurant and then stared back at me with hungry eyes. "I wanted to get here before you could slip out the back and avoid me." A smile twitched at his lips.

"You need a bandage, a cup of coffee, a piece of pie?"

He stalked toward me, pushing my body up against the counter. "Nope. All I need is your forgiveness and a kiss."

Chapter 17

DECKER

My heart hadn't beat this hard or fast in my lifetime. With my body pressed against hers, I waited for some sign that said she'd give me a second chance.

"I heard you that night." Her voice lowered with each word until it became a whisper.

My mind raced with everything I'd said since the day I'd met her. "What did you hear?"

She flattened her hands on my chest, but there was no push. Her palms smoothed over the cotton of my shirt. A surge of want and need gripped my heart and squeezed it like a lemon, sending the acid to my stomach.

"You thought I was asleep, but I wasn't."

"Oh, my God, Hannah." She'd heard me tell her I'd have to give her up. "I was confused. I'd never fallen so hard or so fast for a girl. I was overwhelmed by my father's expectations and my need for you. I thought I had to give one of you up, and since my dad is dying, I chose to keep him for the time being, but it was never my intention to not see you ever again." I lowered my head and touched her forehead with mine. "I'm so sorry."

Her eyes lifted. Her lips were close enough to kiss. "What's changed?"

"Me. I've changed." I lifted her bottom to set her on the counter. "I'm finding a balance." I sat on the stool in front of her and moved her legs so my body could be in my favorite place—right between her thighs. "It's not easy, and it's certainly harder without you as a part of my life."

"How do you know you want me in your life—that you won't change your mind again next week?"

I hadn't considered what I'd do if she turned me away, and that possibility was starting to look likely. My best option was to be bold and be honest. So I yanked her from the counter and sat her in my lap, her legs straddling my waist.

"Because I'm smarter today than I was the other day." I took another chance and pressed my lips to hers. The kiss started tentative, then moved into something more. It wasn't the kind of kiss that had me ripping at clothes to get us both naked. It was more. It was a silent promise that said, *I'm not going anywhere.*

"I'm sorry too. I should have stayed and fought for you. It's that I'm so tired of fighting and losing that I gave up too soon." She nuzzled her lips against my neck.

"Don't give up on me."

"Never."

We kissed for minutes before I pulled away. "Can you get tomorrow off?"

She tilted her head. "Why?"

"Trust me." I was asking a lot since I'd already proved myself to be untrustworthy, but the best advice my father ever gave me was, *If you don't ask, you don't get.* I was putting that logic to the test with Hannah. "I'm playing hooky too."

She pulled out her phone and texted someone. "Done. What's next?"

The diner seemed spic and span, but I didn't want to jeopardize her job. "Should I mop?"

She laughed, and my topsy-turvy world seemed to right itself. "No,

I finished everything before you got here." She ran her hands over her face and hair. "Except for me. I look a mess."

Her face fit perfectly in my cupped hands. "You're beautiful." I climbed off the stool and let her body slide down mine. "Let's go. There's a room waiting for us at the Sonnenalp in Vail."

"You're taking me to Vail?"

"Lock up, sweetheart, time is wasting."

She raced around the restaurant shutting off lights and grabbing the present I'd had delivered today. When we got outside, she looked at her car. "Leave it here. If someone steals it, I'll buy you a new one."

She snorted. "Yeah, right." Her hands brushed over her apron. "I don't have clothes. I have to go home and pack."

Tired of waiting, I picked her up and walked her to the Rover. "You don't need clothes." I gave her a peck on her shocked little mouth. "Whatever you need, I'll supply."

"Where are the cameras? I'm being punked, right?"

I buckled her in, put her present in the back seat, and ran around to the driver's side. "You're being kidnapped. Relax and enjoy. Is there someone you need to call?" I put the Rover in gear and took off toward Vail.

Hannah texted her mom, then turned to me. "I went to see Tanner."

"You too? I showed up at the bar with a bottle of vodka and a broken heart."

Her hand gripped my arm. "You didn't start drinking again, did you?"

I rested one hand on top of hers for a second. "No, I wanted to, but I knew what to do. Buying the alcohol was simply a placebo for drinking it."

"He's helping my mom."

"He's good at helping. She's in good hands. You don't need to worry."

"Worry is my middle name these days. Now that my mom is getting some help, I figured that my life might get back on track. That maybe I could find some balance and go back to school. But then my sister, Stacey, showed up with her jackass boyfriend. She dropped out of school, and she's pregnant."

I reached over the console and held her hand. "You're not her keeper. You can't make decisions for her." I hated that I sounded like my parents, but in hindsight, it was good counsel. "She's responsible for her good and bad decisions."

Hannah let out a loud sigh. "I know, but I wanted one of us to have a good life."

I squeezed her hand. "Why can't it be you?"

She sat in silence for a moment. "You know, you're right. Why can't it be me?"

She fell asleep about halfway through the two-hour drive and woke up as we drove to the valet parking stand.

"Wake up, sweetheart. We're here."

She stretched and looked around at the piece of Bavaria set in Colorado. "It's beautiful."

It was a nice hotel. Nicer yet because I'd never brought a girl here.

The valet opened her door. "Can I take your bags tonight?" he asked.

I rushed around to Hannah. "We don't have any." The valet lifted a brow.

Hannah slugged me in the arm as soon as we were out of earshot. "He thinks we're here for a booty call."

I laughed. "If only I could get so lucky." I walked with confidence to the registration desk. "Riley, checking in."

The woman at the counter looked at me, then at Hannah, and smiled. "Yes, I have you in the signature suite. Can I schedule any spa appointments for you or Mrs. Riley?"

Hannah's expression was priceless. Her plump pink lips fell open. God, it made me want to kiss her. "I'm not—"

"What my lovely wife was going to say is that she's not a morning person, so if we could get a couples massage around eleven, that would be wonderful." I turned my attention to Hannah. "Sound good?"

She pulled her bottom lip between her teeth and nodded.

"Oh, and sadly our luggage was lost. We have nothing to change into. Can you have the boutique send up a selection of clothes to our room so it's waiting for us when we get back from the spa?"

Hannah's smile grew until it was the only thing I saw when I looked at her. I wanted her this happy all the time.

We gave the desk clerk our sizes. I handed over my Amex card, and she handed over the key.

"Let's go, Mrs. Riley," I wrapped my arm around her waist and led her to the elevator. "They have an amazing all-hours menu that includes tea."

She wrapped her arm around my waist and looked at me. "Why are you doing this?"

Didn't she know? "I'm doing this because I like you. More than like you, but more importantly, we both have stressful lives right now, and I thought it would be a nice break if we could just be us for a day or so. I didn't ask you here for sex."

I opened the door into our suite. It was a large room with two beds. I didn't want to assume she'd sleep with me. I was hopeful that I could fall asleep holding her and wake up with her still there. That was my only goal.

"Wow." She walked forward, running the tips of her fingers over all the surfaces, from the green upholstered chairs to the corner fire-place. "This is amazing."

I was used to staying in nice places, so I tried to see it through her eyes, and it was pretty amazing. "Are you hungry?" I knew she was; her stomach had grumbled several times while she was sleeping in the car. "How about I order us some food and you check out the bathtub? If I remember correctly it's a Jacuzzi."

"There's a Jacuzzi?" She spun around, looking for the bathroom entrance. She gripped my hand and dragged me behind her. Smack dab in the center of the bathroom sat the large tub with several dozen bubble jets. "It's big enough for two."

"Is that an invitation?" I dropped her hand and leaned against the marble counter.

"It seems kind of silly for me to take a bath while you wait. Why don't we both enjoy the bubbles, and we'll order room service later, or we'll have a big breakfast in the morning before our massage?"

Dressed in blue jeans and a cotton shirt, Hannah was stunning. Even without a stitch of makeup on, she was the most beautiful woman I'd seen. There was no way I'd turn down an invitation like that.

I pushed off the counter and reached around her body to start the bath, making sure the water was hot enough to relax muscles, but not hot enough to burn.

With my arms crossed, I gripped my shirt and pulled it over my head. Hannah's eyes never left me. I kicked off my shoes and yanked my jeans and boxers down my legs. Naked in front of her, I gave her an eyeful.

Her baby blues widened when my rod hardened and bobbed. Wanting her was a painful endeavor. I palmed myself and stroked it. "You do this to me. All I have to do is think of you, and I'm hard."

She remained silent, but there was a glint of joy in her eyes. "You're not alone." She lifted her shirt and unhooked her bra.

Despite the room being warm and the mirror starting to fog, her nipples beaded tight. Her waist was small, her hips were wide, and every inch of her was perfect. She smelled like strawberries and tasted like honey.

While she continued to undress, I sank into the tub. Seconds later she was completely naked, and all I could do was stare. "Do you have any idea how beautiful you are?" I spread my legs, making a space for her in front of me.

"I know how beautiful I wish I was." She tested the water with her toe and then climbed into the tub in front of me. She fit perfectly between my legs.

"Any more beautiful and I'd have to spend my days guarding you instead of working."

"That sounds good to me." It didn't take long for her to relax against my body.

My hard shaft twitched against her back even though I willed it to go soft. I was back to feeling like a sixteen-year-old seeing his first naked girl. I normally had more control over myself, but not with Hannah. When she so much as walked near me, it stood tall and saluted.

One push of the button and the jets began. Hannah laughed as the bubbles surrounded us. With a squirt of shower gel in my hand, I went to work caressing every inch of her body. Her soft wispy moans spoke to the center of my being. I wanted to lift her up and set her down on me. Instead, I ran my fingers through her slick folds and swirled them around her engorged sex.

"Ohhh," she moaned. "Orgasms are the best stress relief." Her knees fell open and exposed her tender flesh inside and out. In order to gain better access, I lifted one of her legs over the edge of the tub, without thinking about the jets. She hummed when one of the strong streams of water pulsed over her sex.

"Feel good?" Two of my fingers pressed into her tight opening, pumping until she squirmed in my arms.

"Jesus. That's…oh." She tipped her hips up to get the best positioning, and I plunged my fingers in and out of her until she was shaking. Short labored breaths rasped from her mouth followed by my name. Her head fell sideways, and I saw a look of pure bliss wash over her as she came around my fingers. My pace slowed until she stopped shaking and melted into my body.

"I wish you could have seen yourself when you came. Your blonde hair swirled around your head like a halo. Your cheeks blushed, and a look of complete ecstasy softened the tension that lines your forehead. You were ethereal." I wrapped my arms around her body and listened to her breathe.

"Your turn." Her voice cracked.

"Sweetheart, this is all about you." I kissed her on top of her head and pulled us both to a standing position. She wobbled on rubbery legs, but I'd never let her go. Once out of the tub, I rubbed her down with the soft bath sheet and wrapped her like a mummy before I dried myself.

"You are so damn sexy, Decker." She raised one hand and traced down my chest to my stomach. Muscles I'd built by taking my frustrations out in the gym. Her light touch caused a tidal wave of sensations in me that went from my heart to my groin. It would be so easy to pick her up, throw her on the bed, and bury myself inside her, but I wanted to prove to her that she was more than a plaything. And although I planned to play with her all night, tonight was about her satisfaction, not mine.

"Mrs. Riley, what's next?" Although the words were used in play, they didn't seem too far-fetched. I could see Hannah by my side. She seemed to get me when no one else did. She knew firsthand about my addiction, and she was still here with me. And, as a bonus, she didn't judge me because I sucked at riding motorcycles.

"A fluffy pillow and soft sheets sound pretty amazing." She dropped the towel and walked into the living area. Hannah didn't hide behind a bathrobe; she owned her body, and she wore it with confidence. That might have been the sexiest thing about her.

On a counter to the right was a coffee machine. Next to it was a box of tea. "I'm in heaven," my naked angel said while filing through the selections. "Chamomile or mint?"

"I can order freshly brewed from room service." With a towel wrapped around my waist, I walked between the beds and reached for the phone.

"Don't, Decker," Hannah pleaded. "Do you think they are going to do anything different than I will?" She filled the water reservoir up and pressed the start button. Seconds later she had two cups of steaming hot water. "Don't waste your money when we have what we need right here." She dipped tea bags in each cup and picked up a package of cookies that sat in a basket on the bar. "Come sit with me."

After sitting the cups on the nightstand, she climbed onto the right side bed and patted the space beside her.

I dropped the towel and scooted in next to her. She immediately rested her head on my chest.

"What do you want to do when you grow up?" She reached across my body to get her tea.

"I was thinking of quitting my job and becoming your sex slave." We both looked down at my burgeoning erection.

"You're well equipped for that," she said with a dash of sultriness and a tidbit of innocence.

Chapter 18

HANNAH

If he thought we were going to stay in this beautiful hotel and not have sex, the man was insane. "You owe me a do-over."

"I owe you what?"

"You owe me amazing sex that doesn't end with you telling me you can't have me."

"I'm such an idiot. I'm so sorry." He took the teacup from my hands and set it on the nightstand. "Did you say amazing sex?" He rolled over and straddled my legs, pinning me to the soft mattress. His soft kisses tickled my skin from my neck to my breasts. "How amazing do you want it?"

I shimmied down so I was flat on the bed looking up at him. Who would believe that I'd be under this man begging him to make love to me? No wonder the universe had taken Ryker from me. He wasn't Decker, and I'd been waiting for Decker my whole life.

I wrapped my hand around his erection and watched his eyes nearly roll out the back of his head. "I want it so amazing that I'd never consider another."

He sucked my nipple into his mouth. Hot fire raced down my spine to my sex. And although we'd just bathed, I was dripping wet for him.

KELLY COLLINS

My nipple popped from his mouth, and he looked up and smiled. The kind of smile that said *game on*.

"Hannah, I'm going to ruin you for all others." The heat of his mouth trailed down my stomach until he settled between my legs. Slick and hot, he ran his lips up and down my sex, stopping always to pay extra attention to my nub, which had swelled to near bursting. The flat of his tongue felt like sandpaper and satin on my tender flesh.

Just as my knees began to shake and my plunge into ecstasy appeared imminent, he pulled away and started again from the top. First, a long luscious kiss to my lips, followed by a languid lapping at my breasts, and ending with nips and pulls and sucks at my sex until I shook beneath him.

"Not yet, sweetheart." He moved up my body and kissed me again. "I'm going to make love to you, Hannah, because I feel something for you that I've never felt for anyone."

"Hurry, I need you." I gripped his hips and pulled him down toward my body, but he resisted.

"I'm not rushing this." He rolled off the bed and walked into the bathroom. Moments later he was back, and I didn't even pretend not to notice the magnificent sheathed shaft that hung between his legs. My whole body throbbed for him.

I reached forward and pulled him to the bed. His body toppled clumsily over mine, but his rod landed exactly where I wanted it— between my thighs.

"When I'm done, Hannah, you'll know I've been in your body. You'll feel it from your core to your heart. Tomorrow, I better not wake up and find you missing because I'll search for you." He pressed the tip at my entrance, teasing me, making me want him so badly it hurt.

I closed my eyes and bit my lips so I wouldn't scream at him and tell him to take me already.

"Look at me." His voice was husky and full of need. "Just so you know, I'll never be done with you." He plunged into my body with one swift stroke, sending me over the edge.

All that buildup, all that tension eased with one magical plunge,

112

and I wanted more. My nails dug into his thrusting hips. My body rose to meet his. His name left my mouth in a groan.

"It's so good with you, Hannah." He pumped in and out of me. We dripped with sweat, our lungs sucking in whatever air we could gasp. We ground our bodies into each other with a primal need to become one.

My insides tightened and quaked around his thick mass, squeezing and pulsing around him while I dug my nails into his back and hung on for the journey.

"Oh, Hannah, I'm going to come so hard!" he screamed as he threw his head back and shuddered.

He collapsed on top of me, and I was happy to bear the weight. We lay there for a long time as our lips traveled over each other's exposed skin and our hands caressed everything they could touch.

After some time, Decker rolled onto his back and sighed contentedly. "You're killing me."

I rolled over and settled my head on his chest, my arm around his waist, and my leg over his legs. If he thought I was going anywhere, he was wrong. I was in the exact place I wanted to be.

I laughed and hugged him tightly. "We'll die happily together."

"Screw that, let's live happily together. That sounds like more fun." He pulled me on top of his body where his half-hard erection grew stiff as rebar.

"You're ready already?"

He gripped my hips and ground my sex against his length. "Refractory time is for old men. I can go all night." He rolled us over so his body was on top of mine. His eyes were full of playful mischievousness. "We need a new condom." He hopped out of bed and raced to the bathroom.

By round three, his wallet was out of condoms, and I was out of energy, but not out of desire. To my delighted embarrassment, he phoned the front desk and had a new box delivered while I hid under the blankets waiting for round four to begin.

"We're set for the night," he said, waving the strip of condoms in the air like a victory banner.

"Aren't you tired of me yet?" I whispered against the kiss that would start another round.

"Tired…yes. Of you…never." He kissed me deep as he made love to me slowly. His eyes never left mine while he filled me with his passion. "You're my new addiction, Hannah. I don't need a twelve-step program to get over you. You're a habit I never want to kick."

I could have blurted out the words *I love you* so easily. Lying in bed with this man was what I dreamed love would feel like. It was what I wanted love to feel like. Heart. Body. Soul. All bursting full of joy. Did I dare dream of that?

This time, before I drifted off to sleep, I heard different words come from Decker's mouth: "You're mine." Or was that hope creating those words in my head? Maybe it was okay to dream.

MY BODY WAS on fire when I woke up. Not the feverish burn that comes from a virus, but the kind of heat that starts between your legs when a certain sexy man insists on eating you for breakfast.

Decker lifted his face from between my legs. My arousal glistened on his lips. "I ordered you breakfast, but I couldn't wait." He dipped back down and devoured me like I was his last meal. Every bone in my body ached—for more.

He made quick work of getting me to scream his name. Somehow in one night, he'd perfected his technique when it came to my orgasms. He knew where to lick, suck, nibble, pull, and thrust to send me crashing over the edge.

Jelly-limbed, I melted into the bed that had been stripped bare from our sexual acrobatics.

Hard and ready, he bobbed against my stomach when he strad-dled me.

"How much time do we have?" I shifted and sent him falling to the side.

He fell to his back with his pole pointing to the ceiling. "Mrs. Riley, what did you have in mind?"

I loved his playfulness. Coming here was obviously the right thing to do. It gave us both a chance to be ourselves or, in my case, to pretend I was someone else for a moment.

Boldly cupping his sex in my hand, I stroked him from root to tip. "Mr. Riley, I seem to have built up an appetite myself." I leaned over his body and ran my tongue across the thick head, licking up the burst of flavor that had escaped him.

God, how I wished I could have the time to torture him like he did me. Pull him to the edge only to back off and ease him down. To drive him crazy.

I opened my mouth and slid his velvety heat to the back of my throat, then hollowed out my cheeks as I sucked him even deeper. I drew him in and out of my mouth until he gripped my hair and held me in place with his rod probing the back of my throat.

"God, Hannah. That's so damn good. Keep sucking me." His hips fell into rhythm with my mouth until he became needier, greedier, and hungrier to find his release. My head bobbed up and down on his length. My hand gripped his root, pumping him while my mouth pulled at his soft velvety head. He swelled, grew larger than I thought possible, but I kept on working my lips and tongue against his shaft, exploring each vein like it was a map to his pleasure. His orgasm was my only goal.

His hands clutched the fabric of the mattress, and my name slipped from his lips in a sound so pure and sexy that my own sex shuddered in response. His release shot hot and thick across my tongue, and I swallowed it despite my instinct to gag. My eyes watered and my throat burned, but I continued to suck and pull every drop from this man because after today I wanted him to remember that it was my lips that had pulled the best climax of his life from his body.

His body shook until I'd licked him clean. He mumbled words that sang in my heart. *You're mine. So good. You're everything.* Phrases that made me so glad I'd taken a chance on Decker Riley.

He pulled me up his body and hugged me tight to his chest. "I never dreamed that everything I ever wanted and needed could be found in Fury."

A stab of pain pierced my heart because that statement was truer than anything he'd said since we met, yet it had nothing to do with me.

Before I could respond, a knock sounded at the door.

"Room service," a soft female voice called out.

"I got it." Decker bolted from the bed and wrapped the towel he'd discarded last night around his waist. I ran to the bathroom to grab the robe I'd seen hanging behind the door.

When I returned, all covered up, the girl delivering food was gobbling up my man with her hungry eyes.

"There you are, honey," Decker said. "I ordered all of your favorites."

The poor girl deflated like a popped balloon.

"Thanks, baby." I ran my arms around his waist and looked at the girl with an eat-your-heart-out smile. "I think that's all we need." I reached for the warm syrup, scooped up a drop with the tip of my finger, and stuck it into my mouth, giving Decker a look that said he was next on the menu.

He stood with his mouth agape for a minute, then grabbed his wallet for a tip and rushed the girl out the door. The poor thing hadn't cleared the door when he slammed it shut. We could hear her cussing all the way down the hallway.

"Don't be a tease, Hannah."

I yanked the towel from his waist and took in the sight of him. "Don't let other women gawk at what's mine."

"She was gawking? I didn't notice. I only have eyes for you."

I picked up a pancake and flung it at him. It landed against his chest and stuck. "You're so full of shit, but I like the words. Tell me the words again."

He peeled off the pancake and pressed a bite of it into my mouth. "I'm not full of shit. This thing between us is real. Now eat up, sweetheart. We've only got an hour before our couples massage. You're going to need your energy because when we get back, I'm going to press the idea that you're mine solidly into your brain. Whether you're willing to admit it or not, you're the half to my whole."

Chapter 19

DECKER

Massage tables sat side by side with our hands clasped together in between. Never had a moment been so perfect. Hannah moaned each time the masseuse dug deep into her muscles, and it made me hard. Good thing I was lying on my stomach. Otherwise, I'd be sporting a tent no one could miss.

Our heads were turned toward each other. Her eyes had drooped shut minutes ago, worn out from a long enjoyable night.

Love…was this what it felt like? Rather than my heart being filled with torment and regret, was it filled to near bursting with longing? Here we were in the same room, holding hands, and it wasn't nearly enough. I wanted to be connected in every way possible. The closer I was to her, the better I felt about myself.

The sex was phenomenal, but it was more than that. Something about us connected on a level deeper than I could ever imagine.

I reached over and pushed the strand of hair that fell across her face to the side. I needed to see her. So peaceful in her slumber, she was the most beautiful woman I'd ever known, and it wasn't about her looks. I liked her through and through. All the way from her snarky mouth to her tight glove. She was perfect for me because she was so imperfect.

The masseuses' hands left our bodies. They stood by the door while one spoke. "We'll give you a few minutes alone."

I nodded. As soon as they exited the room, I climbed on Hannah's table and pulled her sleeping body into my arms.

She lifted her head from against my chest. "Are we finished?" Her voice was like warm honey dripping over my naked body.

I pressed my lips to her forehead. "With the massage? Yes. With each other? Never." Although I would gladly press myself into her body right now, I knew she was tired and worn out. Last night we'd indulged like love-starved kids. Today I would temper my need for her. Hannah and I had all the days in the world to enjoy each other. We didn't need to make up for years of emotional neglect in one day.

"I'm hungry." Her face lit up with a blush. "For food," she blurted out quickly.

I tried for a crestfallen expression, but all I could do was chuckle. "Of course for food. What else could you mean?"

Her hand reached down and gripped my semi hard erection. "It's been hours since we had sex, and I thought maybe you'd think—"

"That I couldn't live without your mouth or heat around my shaft?" I pulled her body closer to me so we were touching in every place we could. My heart beat out a steady rhythm of happiness. "That statement is true, but I'd trade every blowjob you could give me to hold you like this."

"This is so perfect." She tucked her head close to my chest. "Too bad every day couldn't be like this."

"It could." Her skin was so smooth under my palm. She smelled like lavender with a hint of sweetness that was hers alone. It was a scent that couldn't be bottled. If it could, she'd be rich because I didn't know a man who would be able to resist her.

"Are we still living inside the dream where I'm Mrs. Riley and you're my man?"

She was right. Staying here felt like a dream come true, and it was exactly that: a dream. But I loved living the fantasy, and the great thing about being young was the ability to ignore reality or at least pretend it won't come knocking. "We've still got time." I reluctantly separated my body from hers and climbed off the table. "Let's go eat."

Two robes hung from hooks behind the door. I put mine on and helped her into hers. We left the spa the same way we came in, holding each other's hands.

Just as I'd requested, a clothing rack full of options sat in the center of our suite.

"You were serious?" She stopped dead in her tracks at our door.

"I'm always serious." I led her to the rack. "It's a fault my mom reminds me of often. My father doesn't think I'm serious enough."

"Your father is an idiot." She slapped her hand over her mouth. She immediately turned toward me with eyes full of concern. "I'm so sorry. That was insensitive."

I pulled a pink sundress from the rack and held it in front of her. "What I love about you, Hannah is that you always tell the truth." I slid the robe from her shoulders, and it pooled on the carpet around her feet. "Do you like this?"

She touched the silky fabric and then reached for the price tag. "How much is it?"

I yanked the tag free so she couldn't see it. "The price is irrelevant. I asked if you liked it."

Her frown turned into a scowl. "It may be irrelevant to you, but it's not to me. I'm pretty sure I couldn't afford a button, never mind the entire dress."

"Hannah, I didn't ask you if you could afford it. I asked if you liked it." Although my tone was stern, my smile told her not to take things too seriously. "How many times do I have to tell you I can afford it? In fact, let's take the whole rack." I ran my hands down the twenty or so pieces hanging from the metal bar. "Sweetheart, this is a rounding error in my checkbook."

I pulled a pair of cotton trousers from the rack and pulled them on sans boxers. A perfect fit once I tucked my junk inside. "I was thinking we could have lunch at the fondue place. What do you think?" I chose a light-blue button-down shirt and slipped it on, rolling the sleeves to the area where my gnarly scab began.

"Does it still hurt?" She hung the dress back on the rack and ran her fingertips over my healing wound.

"Not really. You seem to keep my attention elsewhere. I haven't noticed it."

"I'm so glad you crashed your motorcycle, Decker." She reached up on tiptoes and kissed me. "I have to shower this oil off before I wear this dress. I don't want to ruin it."

"Mrs. Riley," I teased, "I'd buy you another one." I swatted her fabulous ass as she walked past me.

One thing about Hannah was she was pretty low maintenance. I'd waited for hours for some women to get ready, but I imagined Hannah would be back in thirty minutes, and I was right. She walked out of the bathroom with her damp hair hanging around her face in waves; her cheeks were pinked by the heat of the water. Her eyes shone clear and happy for the first time in days, and that dress…it was pure sex appeal draped in innocence.

We'd spent the afternoon exploring the town. Everything she stopped to look at, I bought. So what if she didn't need salmon-tooth earrings or chocolate-covered ants? I wanted her to get used to my money.

"Stop buying me stuff I'll never wear, eat, or use." She stood in front of the cashier and begged her to put the chocolate-covered bugs back. "That's gross."

We'd barely made it out the door when her phone rang. "It's Stacey. She's probably thinking someone kidnapped me."

"Hey, Stace. I'm fine, I'm with Decker," she answered. "What? What bad news?" Her pitch hit hysteria in three words. "Oh. My. God."

I had thought we'd be free of drama today. I'd checked in on my father while Hannah was in the shower. He was alive and kicking and not happy I'd taken the day off. I'd ignored his rant and hung up. No one was going to ruin my time with her—no one that I knew anyway.

She ended the call. Her cheeks had lost their pink tone and turned into the sickly color of ash. She looked like she'd drop to the ground any second.

My hands went to her shoulders to steady her. "What's wrong?"

Tears ran from her eyes. "Stacey has been arrested."

"For what?"

"Robbery. I need to get home to get her out. She's pregnant and alone."

"Let's go." I hailed a cab to get us to the hotel quicker. Once there, we collected our belongings and headed back to Fury. Seventy miles an hour was pushing the speed limit, but Hannah was so visibly upset that the risk of a ticket wasn't even a concern. "It's going to be okay." I reached across the center console to hold her hand, but she brushed my hand away.

"Nothing is going to be okay."

Those were the exact words I'd told her days ago, and I'd been wrong. She was wrong, too, but I knew this wasn't the moment to tell her.

"We were stupid. We can't pretend we're other people. It doesn't work that way. We should grow up and be the people we have to be, even if it means we can't have what we want."

"Hannah, that's not true. It might not be easy, but we'll work it out, and it will be worth it."

As soon as I stopped in front of the sheriff's station, Hannah had her hand on the door handle, ready to jump out. "Just go, Decker. I'm not the girl for you. You need someone whose life isn't as screwed up as yours." She left me alone in the car with only her words echoing in my head.

But she was wrong. If she left me, my life would be messed up beyond reason. She was the only thing that made sense.

Chapter 20

HANNAH

I gathered my sister from the sheriff's station where I found her sitting behind Sam's desk eating a burrito like she was enjoying a lunch break.

When we walked outside, Grace was leaning against her car, waiting. Decker, Nate, and Silas were in a huddle off to the side. That was the problem with small towns. Fishbowl living was never private. By supper, the entire town would have some version of the story. It would go all the way from her shoplifting a pack of gum to armed robbery. Fury might not have much, but it had its share of busybodies.

"I can take you home," Grace said.

I looked at my sister. I wanted to hug her and slap her at the same time. Instead, I shook my head. "No thanks. My car is at the diner. Stacey and I need to talk, and the walk will do us good."

Grace gave me a hug and whispered in my ear, "Call me if you need anything."

"I'll take a ride," Stacey piped in, obviously wanting to avoid the guaranteed confrontation.

"You'll walk," I said in a clipped tone that should have left no room for negotiation.

"But I'm pregnant." She placed her hand on her stomach for effect.

"Was that a consideration when you were robbing the gas station?" I gripped her elbow in that place where if you pinched too hard it could fold a person to their knees.

She pulled away with a tug. "I didn't rob the gas station. I left an IOU at the pump."

"You've got to be kidding me. This is all over gas money?" My voice was the type that carried on an average day. Add to that the anger and frustration I felt, and I was sure the entire town of Fury could hear me.

"Wait up." Decker ran to my side. "Let me help."

"I've got it under control." At least Stacey was out of jail, and the crime was a misdemeanor. She'd have her day in court, and she'd get a fine, but at least she wasn't looking at any real jail time … this go-around. With Mark, you never knew what the future held.

"Who are you?" Stacey eyed Decker like he was a window display.

"I'm your sister's boyfriend." He looked at me as if waiting for me to argue.

I had no idea what we were to each other, and I didn't have time to ponder it. "This is Decker."

He offered Stacey his hand, and she took it in a shake that was far too long and friendly for my taste. "Nice to meet you," she said in an uncharacteristic breathy voice.

He paid her no attention, which was one of the things I was beginning to love about him. He was solely focused on his task at hand, and right now that task was me.

"You need to go," I repeated. I felt bad for pushing him away. He was everything I wanted, but I couldn't pull him under the black cloud that hovered endlessly over my head.

His face fell, but he nodded. "The guys need my help with something. I'll stop by your house later with your things." He cupped my cheek and leaned in for a soft kiss. "We need to talk."

He was right. I needed him to understand that this bad luck followed me everywhere. He'd be wise to cut his losses now. "You know where I live?" I asked.

He gave me a slight smile. "I do. I've got connections."

I rolled my eyes. "Understatement." I turned around and marched my sister toward the diner.

Once we were out of earshot, I laid into her. "What the hell were you thinking? If you don't have money, you don't get gas."

Stacey stepped farther away from me. "That's rich coming from the girl who climbed out of a Range Rover minutes ago." She touched the fabric of my dress. "And where did this come from?" She laughed. "That must have been grade-A sex if he bought you a dress."

I wanted to slap the smug look off her face. She had no right to judge me when she'd pulled a Bonnie and Clyde for gas. "I've sacrificed everything for you and Mom. You are such a bitch."

"You sacrificed? I trudged into class every damn day because of you. I gave up Mark two years ago because of you. He begged me to come with him, and I said no because you wanted me to go to college."

"Stacey, he left you anyway. People who love you don't leave you. He's no good for you. Don't forget that I picked you up from the sheriff's station. Speaking of Mark, where was he during all this?"

"He had a meeting at his club, so he left. Sheriff Anders called you and told me to wait. That was illegal, right? He couldn't keep me. I'm over eighteen."

"He was paying you a courtesy. Stop being an ass." I stomped a few feet ahead of her trying to get a block between Decker and me. It would be so easy to run back to him and fall into his arms, and I knew he'd be there to hold me, but how fair was it for me to saddle him with my problems when he had so many of his own? Right now, Stacey was my most pressing problem. If this was what parenting was like, I couldn't blame my mother for numbing herself. "Did you call Mom?"

"No, she left this morning with that guy, Tanner. Maybe he'll keep her, and then we'll both be rid of the burden."

Despite the anger and frustration I'd felt with regard to our mother, I was still compelled to defend her. "She's our mother."

Stacey was at a near run to keep up with me. "Some mother she turned out to be."

Anger coiled inside me. "How did you grow up to be such an ingrate?"

Stacey hopped in front of me and poked me in the shoulder with her finger. "How did you grow up to be such a bitch?"

I fisted my hands and pressed them to my sides. It was all I could do to not punch her. "She's our mother, and let's hope you're as good a mother as she was in her early years."

"You're not setting the bar too high."

I pushed past her. "Are you listening to yourself?"

"Yes, are you? You drive up with your booty call in a fancy Range Rover with a guy that looks like he's walked off the cover of *GQ*, and now you're qualified to give me advice? Wake up, Hannah. Guys like him aren't going to stick around girls like you. They're interested in what's between your thighs, and now that he's had it…well, you know the storyline."

"You're probably right, but at least he talks in full sentences and bathes." I was about to ask whether the day could get any shittier when Cameron Longfellow walked out of the diner. "Why me?" I screamed at the sky.

He stopped dead in my path. "Just the woman I wanted to see." A smarmy smile froze on his face. "I told you I'd see you soon."

Nausea churned in my stomach. Acid burned my throat. How had I ever found him attractive? He had a good-for-nothing look that went perfectly with his overpriced suit and soulless eyes.

"Go screw yourself, Cameron." I flinched, expecting him to hit me again. He didn't. "You need to leave." His presence made my jaw ache the same way it had the day he punched me. Seeing him was like getting hit in the head with a brick.

He held up his hands in surrender. "I'm here to apologize. It's the last thing I have to do in order to be considered cured."

"Great, you apologized, now get the hell out of here."

Stacey eyed Cameron from head to toe. "Who the hell is he?" she asked. "Are you doing all the pretty boys?"

I whirled around to face her. "This isn't your business." I hadn't told anyone in my family what had happened. I didn't want to burden them with my issues when they couldn't even handle their own.

With his hands still raised, Cameron stepped forward. "I never had your sister. She's a teaser, not a pleaser." He lowered his hand and tapped my sister on the nose like she was a four-year-old. "You, on the other hand, might be fun."

I'd had it. Today I was taking Mona's advice. I was putting on my mask first. I fisted up and punched Cameron so hard in the nose he landed flat on his ass.

"I'm pressing charges," he yelled while the blood ran between his fingers to land on his pristine white shirt.

"Because that worked so well for you the last time? I owed you that one. Now stay away from me and my family." I stormed past him to my car. "Get in the car, Stacey."

My sister looked at me, then back at Cameron, who was trying to stand unsuccessfully. She didn't ask another question. Instead, she raced to the passenger side and hopped in.

Miracle of miracles, the car started right up. Once we were on the road, I told my sister everything that happened between Cameron and me.

"Why didn't you say anything?"

I pulled into our overgrown yard and killed the engine. I turned to my sister and sighed. "I didn't want to burden you with my shit. I wanted your mind clear and focused on school."

"I'm sorry to weigh you down with mine." For the first time in a long time, Stacey looked remorseful.

"Are you in love with Mark?" I asked. I picked up my purse and exited the car.

"I'm more in love with the idea of him than him. He's kind of a douche bag, but he's great in bed."

With my arms wrapped around her, I hugged her tight. "He's not father material, Stacey. You have to think about your baby."

"You're right. That's what started it all. I spent my last twenty bucks on a home pregnancy test, and he was pissed."

I shook my head, hoping I heard her right. "You don't know for sure if you're pregnant?"

She shrugged. "I feel bloated, and I'm late." She reached into the paper bag and came out with an unopened First Response box. "Let's go inside and see if you're going to be an aunt."

We walked inside, and she went straight to the bathroom.

She spoke through the door while she peed on the stick. "Can you believe he pumped the gas and took off?"

"He what?"

"He left me there with no money and no way to pay, so I wrote an IOU and stuck it on the pump handle before I started to walk back. That's when Sheriff Anders swung by and picked me up. Roy had called in the theft."

I leaned against the wall and waited for what seemed like an hour but was minutes. "So how did Silas and Grace end up at the sheriff's office?"

She opened the door with a smile on her face and breezed past me toward the kitchen. I wasn't sure whether that meant positive or negative. I didn't have a good handle on where her feelings were concerning Mark. They seemed to have a love-hate thing going on. "They showed up with Nate and a bag full of burritos. Which was awesome because I was hungry."

She grabbed for the teapot, and I gripped her hand. "Stacey, what the hell did it say?"

"I'm not pregnant."

I wanted to jump to the heavens, but I also didn't want to be insensitive. "How do you feel about that?" That was one of the first phrases I learned in my psychology class.

She lit the gas burner under the kettle and walked to the table where she plopped down onto a chair. "I don't know. Relieved. Pissed at myself that I even considered having his baby. He doesn't love me. Once he bailed on me today, I realized he only loves what I bring to his life, which is occasional cash and a willing body when he strolls through town."

"What now?" I took the chair across from her. "Do you want to go back to school?"

"God no, I hated school. It's pretty bad when Mark seemed like a better alternative."

"You should have told me." My hand rested on top of hers.

"I didn't want to disappoint you."

Uncontrollable laughter bubbled up inside of me. "We are quite the pair. I want desperately to go back to school, and you were willing to get pregnant to escape it."

"We *are* a pair. You have a super-hot boyfriend, and I attract men who are worse than maggots."

I got up to make an ice pack for my bruised hand. "I've had my share of maggots." The cold pressed to my knuckles hurt like hell, but it hurt in the best of ways. "You know, Decker isn't my boyfriend. He's…I'm not sure what he is."

"He's in love with you. I saw the hurt in his eyes when you told him to leave. It's a good thing that Silas and Nate were going to find Mark to beat him up, otherwise, I'm pretty sure your puppy would have followed you all the way to the car."

"They're going to what?" I reached for my phone to text Decker.

"That Silas guy has a real problem with men mistreating women. He said he was going to teach Mark a lesson. I only hope it's super painful."

"Oh, shit," I said as I sent a *where are you* text.

Chapter 21

DECKER

K icking someone's ass wasn't my average pastime. I was more of a lover than a fighter. In fact, I couldn't remember a time I had ever hit anyone, but I was game to tag along with Nate and Silas. Maybe I could keep them out of jail or out of the hospital. At the least, it kept me near people I felt a strange kinship to, and it gave me a reason to not visit Dad in the ICU. My daily visits were riddled with emotions that ran the gamut from regret to rage. And now that I hadn't shown up for work for two days, he'd be furious.

Dad would never understand the need to set a man straight for wronging a woman. He'd never put his neck on the line for anyone else, family included. Dad was more of a survival-of-the-fittest type of guy. A real Darwinian cultist. Only the strongest survived. And the strong tended to be savvy swindlers like him.

As for women, I would never hurt one physically or emotionally—on purpose. I'd taken the upfront approach all my life. I'd always told them it was a swipe-right date—simply a hookup. If they thought they could change my mind, they were lying to themselves. That was until I met Hannah. She was not a swipe-right chick, she was simply right. She was unlike anyone I'd dated before. She wasn't refined. She wasn't rich. She wasn't over-educated. Hannah was real, and I liked real.

"You ready?" Silas asked. He looked at my clothes. "Hope you're not attached to that outfit, there's a real chance you're going to get dirty."

"I've been dirty before." I rolled up my sleeves and showed off the beef-jerky texture of my still-healing arm. Every move made the scab crack and bleed. I might have grown up wealthy, but I didn't grow up a wuss.

"I'll drive." I led the two men to my Ranger. It still smelled like Hannah's perfume. After one long inhale, I was ready to face anything. "Tell me what's going on so I'm up to date."

Silas and Nate tag-teamed the story of Hannah's sister and the man she'd fallen for. I knew a lot of other men who were also the love-them-and-leave-them type, but the difference between them and me was the disclosure part.

In college, my roommate often went what he'd called "slumming," which meant he preyed on women of lesser means. He enticed them with promises of more, and they fell for it. Yet in the end, when women compared the two of us, I was known as the asshole because I'd been honest with my intentions and he'd been the one that got away.

"What's going on between you and Hannah?" Nate sat in the center of the back seat and leaned forward.

How did I explain what I didn't understand myself? "I like her. She's a good girl." I wanted to slap myself up the side of the head. *She's a good girl?* I sounded like a stupid camp counselor giving a parent an update.

"Don't hurt her. She's had enough shit happen in her life." His voice was dead calm, but there was more than a hint of a warning in it.

I chanced a glance back to see whether there was some expression that would tell me about his relationship with Hannah. Were they friends? Past lovers? "I never go into a relationship with the intent to hurt."

"Turn right at the highway and head all the way past Pine Creek. I'm told Mark hangs out at Getty's," Silas said.

"What's the plan when we get there?" I was brought up to plan. My life had been planned out since the day I was born. Planning amounted to success. If we were going to kick ass, I wanted to be on the winning side.

"No plan, we'll have a chat with Mark." Silas explained that they handle things a certain way in small towns, especially the bikers. If I cared about Hannah, then I'd help her sister, and that meant showing Mark he couldn't mess with her.

Nate, although dressed like Barbie's Ken, stretched his arms over the seat and flexed his fists. "I'm itching to kick some ass." Knuckles cracked beside me. "If we get rid of Mark, then maybe there's a chance for me. I've had a crush on Stacey for a long time."

Silas whirled toward the back seat. "What the hell happened to Melissa?"

"She wasn't interested in me, only my bedroom skills." The soft leather ate up any noise Nate made when he fell back against the cushion. "I bet you get that a lot." Nate kneed the back of my seat so I knew he was talking to me. "Except it's probably about your money and not your junk."

I swerved the car so he'd feel it. "Don't discount my junk. I haven't had anyone get up and leave once they saw it." Why were men so protective of their dicks? You didn't see women wagging their breasts in public, comparing size. Oh, wait—you did. In fact, women were worse.

"I'm not asking you to whip yours out and show me, all I'm saying is you probably have to ask yourself why women want you."

Silas broke in with, "What Nate's saying is, guys like us have nothing to offer women as far as money. So when a woman falls for us, it's got to be our pricks or our charming personalities."

"You have a wife, right?" I didn't have the 411 on Silas. I only knew that he had a woman and a child. That much I got from Hannah. And from how he rushed over to a redhead named Grace and kissed her before we left.

Silas sat taller. "I've got Grace and Blue. We're engaged, and if she'd let me, I'd rush her to the courthouse tomorrow and get it all in writing, but she insists on taking off her baby weight before she says I do."

"She looks great to me." Nate ducked when Silas tried to back-hand him.

"Keep your eyes off my woman," Silas growled at Nate and then turned to me. His eyes lit on me like an interrogation lamp. "Is this thing with Hannah serious?"

What could I say: *I buried myself in her body, and I never want to live anywhere else?* That sounded superficial and lame, but it was true.

"It's early."

"Screw early." Silas laughed. "The first kiss with Grace and I was sunk."

Nate sat forward again. "It's because you're a pussy. And I thought you were this tough-ass, eat-ants-for-breakfast Special Forces guy. One kiss from a girl and you become one."

"The right girl can make a difference." The cab went silent with my admission. "I kissed Hannah, and it was different from anything I've experienced."

Nate let out a snorting kind of laugh. "When I kissed Hannah, all I felt was yuck."

Instinct had me slamming on the brakes. A horn sounded behind me as I pulled to the side of the road. "You kissed Hannah." My knuckles gripped the steering wheel until they turned white. "When were you kissing Hannah?" White-hot jealousy threaded through my body and lodged in my heart, where it hurt like hell to hear that another man's lips had been on my woman. That's right, my woman. Hannah was mine.

It took everything in me to not climb in the back seat and beat the human man Barbie to a pulp for touching Hannah.

"Dude, calm down." Nate rested his hand on the door handle, ready to bolt if needed. "She kissed me, but not because she liked me. She kissed me to make Ryker jealous. She had this long unrequited-love thing going on for him, but Ana stole his heart. You want to beat anyone's ass, go after Ryker."

The heat kept building up inside me as I pulled back onto the highway. "Did your brother date my Hannah?" Now I sounded like a father trying to make a man do right by his daughter. I was fifty flavors of messed up when it came to her.

"You're in love with her." It was hard to miss the shit-eating grin covering Silas's face.

"I like her." I defended my position. "Love? Hardly. How can I love someone after such a short time?" That wasn't an attempt at deflection. It was a question I'd been asking myself all day. Yet in my heart, I knew I'd truly experienced something different and real with Hannah.

"I lied to myself too." Silas slapped me on the back. "You'll figure it out, little brother."

Right then, I wished I hadn't been an only child. What would it have been like to have brothers to share life's experiences with?

Getty's came into view over the last hill. It was perfect casting for a *Sons of Anarchy* episode or maybe a *Wild Hogs* scene. The problem was, I was more like William H. Macy, Silas was a dark-haired version of Jax and Nate? He was a young Tim Allen in nicer clothes. We were an eclectic mix of rich boy, bad boy, and pretty boy.

"Are we talking or fighting?" Nate asked. "I need to know if I should leave my watch here or wear it." He unbuckled his Rolex knockoff and tucked it under the seat. "I suppose some fist action is warranted."

We sat in the car for a moment while the guys filled me in about Hannah's sister's boyfriend. I didn't tell anyone that she was pregnant because it wasn't my story to tell, but any man who would put the mother of his child at risk deserved an ass-beating.

"Let's do this." Silas pushed open the door and climbed out. For a second, I put myself in Mark's place and almost felt sorry for the man. I hadn't met him, but there was no way he could stand up to Silas's bigger-than-life presence.

In the little time I'd known him, I'd gotten the distinct impression that he fought for the underdog. I respected that about him. And after seeing him with his brother, Ryker, I envied them for the bond they shared.

Side by side, we walked into the bar like cowboys in an old

spaghetti western. There were no revolvers strapped to our hips or spurs on our boots, but we carried ourselves like outlaws walking into a saloon.

The lights were dimmed, and the room smelled of stale cigarettes and mold. Silas scanned the space. It was interesting to watch him survey the surroundings. He was out of the Army, but he was still a soldier through and through. His eyes shifted from place to place as if assessing the situation. Defining the danger. Planning a way forward and considering an escape.

At the bar sat three bikers, tatted up from their wrists to their leather cuts. A female bartender leaned over the old wooden surface. Her breasts spilled over the top of her shirt like an offering. The edge of a twenty-dollar bill poked from her exposed bra.

Nate nodded toward a corner table where one man sat alone. He fit the description. Tall, light-haired, and lanky with a hint of cowardice and a dose of stupidity.

"Drink?" The woman tending bar called over to us.

"No thanks," Nate said. "We're here for something else."

Silas shook his head. "He's still learning the way of the world. We'll take three beers."

I almost changed his order but decided it was best to not draw more attention to us. We weren't the group from *Easy Rider*. We were two idiots with a point to prove and a getaway driver.

"You Mark?" Silas swung a chair around and straddled it, coming to sit beside the solitary man.

"Who's asking?"

I watched with fascination as Silas leaned in and spoke with calm. "A friend."

Mark tensed and sat up, giving himself three more inches in height, but he didn't come close to Silas. In fact, none of us lacked in that department.

"You're not my friend, so what do you want?"

Not one bit riled, Silas leaned back and rose to his full-seated height. Mark's eyes widened. It was one thing to look at a man sitting next to you and feel superior, but when you lined them up, you couldn't compare them apples to apples. Mark was more like a grape whereas Silas was a grapefruit.

"I'm here for Stacey."

Mark looked like he'd swallowed fermented fish guts. "She's a waste of time and sperm." He threw back his beer and slammed his bottle on the table. "Bad decision. Bad lay. Bad everything."

Tension rippled through the air. The bartender approached with three opened bottles.

Nate moved forward. "She's no longer your concern."

Mark laughed. It was the kind of cackle heard before a psycho stabbed his victim. "You gang-banging the whore? You seem a little tame for her. She likes the bad boys." His eyes settled on Silas. "As long as sloppy seconds are your style, go for it. Just know that I'm not paying a penny for the little whelp I planted inside her."

Nate sprung forward. "She's pregnant?" His fist connected with Mark's nose. The crack echoed through the air. A moment of silence soaked into the bar, and then all hell broke loose.

Nate was pummeling Mark's face when the three men from the bar entered the melee. One fisted my collar and threw me into the wall. The sheetrock folded behind my head. A sharp edge ripped into my scalp.

Silas fended off two men while the one who tossed me aside went after Nate. Two on one was unfair in any book, so I pushed off the wall and threw myself into the fray despite the blow I'd taken.

The first punch that connected to my face sent my adrenaline racing. Once the initial sting wore off, I didn't feel a thing. In fact, each punch I threw released years of pent-up frustration and anger. I didn't see my father's face behind any punch. I saw something less tangible. Each hit was retaliation for a life not lived authentically.

In the background, the bartender's high-pitched scream floated above us, not connecting with everything happening. This was more than a bar fight. This was justice. It was redemption. And when the door swung open and Ryker stepped in, it was over.

The man plowed through the fight like a bowling ball on a strike mission.

"Jesus, Silas." Once all the men were on the floor and the

bartender was cowering in the corner, Ryker looked at me and lit into his brother. "What the hell did you bring him here for?"

His dismissal stung. He'd set me aside like I didn't belong, and it pissed me off. "He didn't bring me. I drove." I swiped at the sweat running down my forehead only to find out it was blood and that it streamed steadily from a gash to my head.

I reached for the table as the room began to spin. "What kind of brother are you?" Ryker yelled at Silas before everything turned black.

Chapter 22

HANNAH

I paced the floor at Boulder General Hospital, waiting for word on Decker. After the call came from Ryker, I rushed right over. I wasn't the only one.

The waiting area filled up as one by one, the people of Fury started to show. Ana and Grace came first. Ana wrapped her arms around a worried Ryker. He pulled her and Wren into his arms. I no longer felt jealous of what they had; I felt inspired to find that for myself. Something told me Decker would be the pot of gold at the end of my journey.

Grace sat Blue's baby carrier on the floor beside her and punched Silas in the arm. Then she pulled him into her arms and kissed him.

Everyone was paired up except Nate and me. Grace with Silas. Ana with Ryker. Mona with Marty. Even my mother showed up with Tanner. There was a light in her eyes that had been snuffed out years ago. Despite the somber situation, I felt a sparkle of hope for her.

That spark was quickly extinguished, at least for the moment, when Ryker separated Silas from the crowd and pushed him into a corner. "You messed up big-time." His voice wasn't tempered for the crowd. It came out full force like an angry storm.

Silas touched the cut on his lip, making it bleed again. "You should have seen him." A look of pride replaced the grimace of pain. He swiped a tissue from the table to stanch the slight blood flow. "He's like us, Ryker. He jumped in when things got hot. He's a Savage all the way to his bones. We have to tell him who he is."

Ryker looked at me for a second, then turned the full force of his agitation on Silas. "Make up your mind. You're like a ping-pong ball. Tell him. Don't tell him. What's it going to be?" Ryker swiped at the drop of blood on Silas's lip. "Is this what you want for him? You want to bail him out of bar fights and rush him to the hospital?" Ryker shoved his hands into his pockets. "He's got at least a half-dozen stitches coming."

"He'll survive!" Silas yelled back. "He wasn't born into Range Rovers and Rockport shoes, asshole. I'm telling you. He's a nature-beats-nurture poster child."

The way Ryker towered over Silas sent a skitter of fear up my spine. I looked over at Ana, who knew him best, but there wasn't a speck of fear in her eyes. She trusted him.

Grace, on the other hand, looked like she was in Ryker's corner. It was obvious she was pissed at Silas. It showed from her punch to his arm to the crossing of hers.

Tired of the chaotic emotions swirling inside me, I marched to the two brothers who were in a standoff.

"Stop! Both of you!" I yelled like an elementary school teacher breaking up a recess fight. "You can argue about this later, but right now, all he needs is your support. I don't care if it comes from the position of a friend or a family member, get yourselves in gear and figure it out."

Both men stared at me like there was nothing more frightening than me. And I supposed they were right. I'd glanced at myself in the mirror. With hair that looked like I'd been caught in the eye of a tornado and eyes shadowed by exhaustion, I was a mess. Like a woman gone mad.

I marched toward Tanner and Mom.

"How come I don't know about this boy, Hannah?"

I shook my head. "Welcome to reality, Mom. I'm so glad you woke up."

"I'm so sorry, sweetheart." She cupped my cheek, and I wanted to cry, but there was no time.

"Is there a Hannah here?" a pink scrub-clad nurse called from the doorway.

I raised my hand and headed that way.

"That's me."

The nurse named Amber walked a few paces ahead of me. "There's a handsome young man asking for you."

It warmed me inside knowing that of all the people in the waiting room, Decker wanted to see me first.

We turned into a room, and sitting in the bed looking black and blue but devastatingly handsome was Decker. The white bandage taped to his forehead didn't detract from his features at all. Kind of made him sexy in a bad-boy way.

"There you are. Come here." He patted the bed beside him. "I wasn't sure if you knew I was here, but then the nurse said I had an entire fan club waiting, and I hoped you were in it."

I rushed to the side of his bed and pulled a chair close.

He moved his head side to side. "Not close enough. Come up here with me." He reached for my hand and pulled me into his lap.

"I'm going to hurt you." My attempt to wiggle away was futile. Decker held on to me like I was glued to him.

"It will hurt me more if you're not right here where I want you." He pressed his swollen lips to mine and winced.

"You're a worse mess than me." I ran my fingertips over his bandage. "I'm so sorry. This is all my family's fault."

Decker sat in silence for a moment, stroking my hair. "Family is a funny concept. You can be part of one and feel disenfranchised, or you can be with people who have no ties to you and feel this great connection."

My arms naturally circled his body, and my head rested comfortably on his chest. "Why you guys got involved, I have no idea."

"Because we love you, and so we love those you love." He pushed me away and stared. "I love you, Hannah. I don't know how it's possible, but I know why."

All the words I wanted to say rose up and choked me. The only word that got free was, "Why?"

The starched sheets crinkled beneath us as he shifted my body to straddle his. He cupped my face in his palms. "Because when I'm with you, I feel everything."

"Can I confess something?"

He lifted a bruised brow. "I thought we had all our dark secrets out in the open already."

I nibbled my lower lip. Too bad that wasn't true. I knew one of his dark secrets. I knew who he was. And I still hadn't told him. Part of me didn't believe it was my job. Another part of me wanted to be the one to give voice to the reason he felt disconnected. His life was a lie, but like the other Savage boys, I found it hard to tell the truth when you weren't sure which life would be better for him.

"I'm in love with you." There. It was out in all of its silliness. How could someone who'd been so burned fall in love in such a short period?

He whispered against my lips, "Don't keep that a secret from me. I need to hear those words more than you'll ever know."

"I love you, Decker, from the bloody bandage on your head down to your crooked pinky toe."

It pained me to kiss him. I felt his pain like he lived inside of me. It had to have hurt his split lip to press against mine. His bruised and bloody knuckles had to have ached with every squeeze he gave my waist, and his head must have pounded with every beat of his heart.

"My crooked toe, huh? That has to be love."

I slid from his lap and curled up next to his body. My eyes were drooping shut after a long night...,but they snapped open when a woman rushed into Decker's room.

"Decker, what the heck happened? I've been worried about you." A dark-haired woman dressed for high tea hovered over us. Her hands flew to his face. "Look at you."

"Mom, I'm all right."

This wasn't how I imagined meeting his mother. In fact, I hadn't given the scenario much thought. Was I the type of girl Decker brought home? With his wealth and position, I imagined not. When

I closed my eyes and envisioned Decker and another woman, it was like lancing my own gut with a rusted, dull blade. But in all honesty, I didn't see him with someone like me. His girl would have had a golf club or a mimosa in her hand, not an order pad or a butter knife.

He said he loved me, but could I trust that? Maybe he had a savior complex, and I was his next project.

His arms pulled me closer, and I wasn't sure whether he was shielding me or I was shielding him.

Finally, his mother noticed he wasn't alone. Her eyes fell to my face. "Are you Hannah?"

Her knowing smile immediately destroyed every shred of doubt that had burrowed inside me minutes ago. My heart soared free, but only for a second.

Those old seeds of doubt returned as fast as they'd vanished, digging into my skin like a splinter and threatening to fester inside my fleeting sense of calm. Maybe it was John who told her.

I lifted my head from Decker's chest and faked a heart-warmed smile. "I am Hannah. You must be Decker's mom."

She didn't give me stink eye or look at me like I was some gutter tramp. A genuine grin crossed her face. "I'm so excited to meet you. Although—" She gave Decker an accusatory look. "—I would have preferred that it not be in the hospital."

After inching myself free from Decker's hold, I slid off the bed to my sandaled feet. I was still dressed in the pretty pink sundress he'd bought me. I wondered what she'd think of me if she saw me dressed for my normal world, in worn blue jeans and an apron.

"I should be going so you two can talk. It was nice meeting you, Mrs. Riley." Saying her name created warmth from the memory of the moments I pretended to be the same.

Decker's head was already shaking. He held his hand out to me, but I remained out of reach.

It was his mother who caught me by the arm. "You don't need to go, sweetheart." She pulled me to her side. "For goodness' sake, call me Peggy."

"I really do need to go. I have an early morning shift, and I still need to take care of a few things. Besides—" I looked at the man I knew I loved, "—he has a fan club waiting outside to see him."

I broke free of her touch and walked toward the door. Like a mime, I lifted a fake phone to my ear. "Call me once you've rested."

I was only a step out the door when I heard his mom say, "Your father is fading fast, but he's been asking for you. Where have you been?" I stopped for a second to listen.

"Clearing my head. Spending time with Hannah. Thinking about my future."

"This must be so hard for you," his mother crooned, and I could almost see her sitting on the edge of the bed and pulling him in for a hug.

Feeling guilty for eavesdropping, I left and joined the others in the waiting room.

All eyes were on me when I entered. "He's going to be okay."

A collective sigh was heard throughout the room.

"Marty," Mona said, "we're out of here, then. I need pie and coffee in that order." The two had become connected at the hip—Marty's bad hip. What a pair they were. She was blind, and he used a walker. I wasn't sure who was in worse shape, but they went together like spaghetti and meatballs. One was less without the other.

I hugged the old couple. Mona always smelled like melted chocolate while Marty was mothballs dipped in Old Spice.

"Are you taking care of yourself, young lady?" Despite her macular degeneration, Mona still managed to cast a meaningful glance at the exact location where my mom sat with Tanner.

"Yes, ma'am. My mask is safely secured for the first time in a long time."

She lifted her dark glasses and looked into my eyes. At least I imagined that was where she was focused. It was hard to tell. "You're going to be okay. My question is … will that boy be once he learns the truth?"

That was the million-dollar question, and I couldn't answer it.

Chapter 23

DECKER

Mom stayed while my friends funneled into the room. She said hello to each one and cooed at the babies.

Ryker and Silas approached her and apologized for the fight as if it were somehow their fault. As the details came to light and Mom got a good idea of where and how the event transpired, her smile turned into a frown. I got the feeling that there was more to her concern than the fact I had eight stitches in my head.

"I'm going to your father. You need to come soon." Usually warm and friendly, Mom's clipped tone caught me by surprise, and I found myself apologizing for the first time in my life for her behavior after she left.

"She's worried." Ana said as she bounced her chubby baby on her hip. Grace held Blue to her chest and kissed his red hair. Ryker and Silas stood by their women, and I could feel the sense of belonging that weaved through this group.

Nate leaned against the wall. Two black eyes were already forming, and I was sure his nose would never be the same. "I'm heading out." He raised his hand in the air and groaned. "Shit, that hurt."

"Come by the shop tomorrow. Your bike's ready?"

"His bike?" Tanner asked. He and Hannah's mother had been

standing off to the side, holding hands. Weird that the man who'd been there the most for me was hanging out with the woman who hadn't been there for Hannah. I was glad because Tanner made a difference in people's lives, and it had nothing to do with selling them a bunch of shit they didn't want or need.

"Yes, the Harley Fat Boy I crashed the night I met Hannah." Best damn night of my life and not nearly as painful as the stitches in my head.

Everyone nodded like it was normal to crash a bike into a tree, and maybe in Fury it was, or maybe it was expected from a guy like me. No matter what, I was determined to learn how to ride that beast. Like Hannah, it was something that I knew was part of my soul.

Once everyone left, I made my way slowly down to the ICU. In the hallway, I leaned my tired body against the doorjamb and looked at the man who had been bigger than life. His once strong and imposing frame had withered away to that of a much older, weaker man.

I wasn't sure how it was possible for Dad to look any worse than he had days ago, but time seemed to ravage him with speed and efficiency. His skin had taken on the pallor of death.

"Decker's here, honey." Mom patted the crepey skin of Dad's hand.

He looked in my direction. His once bright eyes were as orange as the jelly candies Mom ate around Halloween. "Decker, come here." His words rattled deep and wet. His eyes settled on the bandage on my forehead. "If you'd stayed focused and at work, you wouldn't be hurt."

I touched the strip of gauze and felt the throb of the injury pulse under the bandage. The wound beneath didn't hurt as much as his words. Never a word of encouragement.

I pushed off the doorjamb and stalked forward. "What is it with you? I've given everything to make you happy. Nothing works. It's never worked. You're going to die disappointed in me, and I'm going to have to live with the fact that you hated me."

"I don't hate you, Decker. I …" He coughed and coughed until the nurse came in to check on him. She hit the morphine button and

144

left. Dad looked up at me with vacant eyes. The kind that drifted to another place even when they were focused on something else.

"I'm drowning here, Dad. You what? Hate me?" I shoved my hands into my pockets, afraid I would reach for him and shake the words from his graying lips. "How do you hate your own flesh and blood? I'm your son, for God's sake."

Dad struggled to sit up. His eyes drooped, but in them I could see the determination to get the last word said. He looked at my mom. "You have to tell him, Peggy. He needs to know."

Mom's head fell to the bed, and she started to cry. When she looked at me, the sadness in her eyes was like a knife to my heart.

The scene was like walking into a horror movie. Everyone around me held a bloody knife, and I had no idea who had stabbed me, but intuition told me it would get worse before it got better.

"What the hell is everyone talking about?" I yelled.

The nurse walked by, reached in, and shut the door.

With what looked like his last ounce of energy, Dad said, "You're not my son."

Only the beeps of monitors broke the silence. Mom's tears stopped, Dad slipped into his drug-induced sleep, and the floor fell out from beneath me. My long legs collapsed. I reached for the wall to help soften the fall and sat on the polished floor, feeling dulled from the pain of years of betrayal.

"Decker…"

I held up my hand to stop her from talking. I needed to make sense of the words. To make sense of the moment. To make sense of my life.

"He's not my dad?" All the hurt I'd experienced over the years swallowed me. I leaned against the wall for support. "Who's my father?"

Mom tucked the covers up to Dad's neck and leaned in to kiss him. "I'll be back," she whispered. She stood above me and held out her hand. "Come home, Decker. There's a lot to explain."

THOSE FOUR WORDS, "You're not my son," changed everything and nothing.

Mom made tea while I fidgeted with the fake fruit in the bowl on the table.

While Mom usually took the seat next to me, tonight she sat across from me with a manila envelope pressed so hard to the surface of the table her fingertips blanched.

"Are you hungry?" Mom's voice shook.

"Stop stalling, Mom. I need to know everything you're keeping from me." I scrubbed my hands over my face, trying to pump some life into my deadened nerve endings.

She rubbed the envelope like it was mink. "First off, you need to know that your father loves you."

"Which father is that? The one lying in the hospital bed that I manage to disappoint more than please, or the one who impregnated you?"

She flinched at my harsh words. "Let me start at the beginning."

"Perfect," I said with a large dose of sarcasm.

She let out a deep rattling sigh. "Your dad … Rip has always been an overachiever. It's in his core to succeed at everything, but he couldn't produce a child."

"So he's sterile, and he blamed it on you?"

"No, that was my idea. I came up with the hard labor story so you didn't question not having siblings. That's not the point." Mom's head shook side to side. "The point is, that as an overachiever, he couldn't give me the one thing I wanted—a child."

"Okay, at least I know why he never warmed up to me."

"Decker, you're missing the point. He failed me. Rip Riley can't deal with failure, so even though you didn't share his DNA, he was determined to make you his in every other way, but he couldn't make you love real estate the way he did. Another failure on his part, in his eyes."

"Shit, Mom. He doesn't love real estate. He loves the art of the deal. He loves the kill. He loves the money."

"He loves you too. He doesn't understand where he went wrong." Mom wrung her hands together with them hovering over the mysterious yellowed envelope. "He wanted you to have his passion."

"He shoved it down my throat every day. I've lived, slept, and breathed real estate since I was born. While my classmates headed to summer camp, I was stuck in ethics training with people three times my age."

Mom shifted in her seat. "And look at how good you are with people."

I slapped my hand on the table, making a fake orange jump from the bowl and roll off the edge. "I was thirteen. Let's cut the crap, Mom. Who is my father? Have I met him? Does he hate me too, or did you use an anonymous sperm donor?" All the scenarios raced through my aching head.

She took a lifetime to answer. "As far as DNA goes, I am not your mother either."

Her words hit me like a sledgehammer. "What the hell?" Every truth I'd known was a lie, and I couldn't catch my breath or stop the world from spinning around me.

"Decker, you will watch your mouth. I may not have given birth to you, but I raised you. You will not disrespect me or your father."

I hung my head, and for the first time in years, I cried. That was something I was never allowed to do. Crying showed weakness, and Rileys weren't weak. But it turned out I wasn't a Riley. "Were you ever going to tell me?"

I saw the answer in her eyes before she uttered the words. "No. There was no reason." She slid the envelope across the table. "Before you open it, you need to know that your early life ended in tragedy." She shuddered. "Your parents were murdered."

A lump the size of Texas lodged in my throat. "How old was I when you adopted me?" I covered the envelope with my hand.

"Eight months old. You were the cutest, sweetest thing ever. Your dad and I could tell that you were loved by your birth parents. You were so easy and so happy."

"What's in here?" I slid my finger under the edge of the envelope and opened it slowly.

"Everything. It's all there." Mom took the folder from my hands and pulled out a packet of papers. "When you started to go to Fury, I worried. You were getting too close to the truth."

My mind raced to the tiny town I felt so comfortable visiting. "My parents died in the massacre there?"

Mom's eyes filled with tears. "Yes." She looked to the packet of papers and set them before me. "You have brothers. We couldn't take them. How could we go from no children to three? I'm so sorry."

I sucked in lungfuls of air, hoping the oxygen would keep me conscious as everything dimmed to darkness around me. I grappled for my tea and took a drink.

"I have brothers?"

Mom lifted from her seat and came around the table to hug me. "Decker, I loved you like my own. I will always love you. I thought we'd be enough. I never imagined you would have to know. That's my mistake. I'm sorry."

I didn't know what to say. I couldn't deny that she'd loved me. She was the one constant in my life that I never questioned. "I love you too, Mom. That will never change."

"I'll leave you alone for a few minutes. I'll be out back if you want to talk about it." She walked away. I waited for the click of the sliding glass door before I picked up the packet of papers.

I read through the first page, which was legal mumbo jumbo decorated with a Records Sealed stamp. The second page had my vital statistics. At least they hadn't changed my birthdate. For that matter, they hadn't changed my first or middle name, but when I got to the last name, I was paralyzed. Decker Owen Savage. *Could it be?* No wonder Dad disliked bikers so much. I'd been born into a family of them.

I gripped my keys and walked out the front door.

It took me an hour to get to Fury and another thirty minutes of stopping everyone to ask them whether they knew where the Savages lived.

Standing on the doorstep of Ryker and Ana's home, I raised my hand to knock and lowered it several times. *Did they know?*

My phone buzzed in my pocket for the second time. It was Mom asking where I'd gone.

I'm okay. I love you. I need a few days to process, I texted back.

My heart beat so fast I feared it would give out with the exertion. Once they opened the door, what could I say? *Hey man, I'm your long-lost brother?*

I turned around to leave, and the door cracked open. "Decker?" It was Ana.

"Hey, I was in the neighborhood and I thought I'd stop by and say hello." What kind of fool was I? *Just in the neighborhood* worked for people who lived in the next town over, not an hour away.

She stepped back and opened the door wide. "Come in. Ryker is putting Wren to bed. I'll get him."

"I don't want to bother your family." What was I saying? I was their family; they didn't know yet. Or did they?

"Don't be silly." She reached for my hand and tugged me inside. "Make yourself comfy. I'll be right back." She disappeared down the hallway.

I stood in the center of their living room. The walls were covered in photos and birds. Actually, photos flanked by birds. My eyes ran the length of the room until I came to an old photo of a happy family—two parents and three boys. And there was no doubt I was the baby.

Upon further reflection, I realized that I'd never asked about newborn pictures. Our hallways were covered with photos of me from late infancy—which must have been the time Mom adopted me—to now. She called it her wall of love, and it left me with no doubt that she cherished me. If I was on Ana and Ryker's wall of love, did that mean they too would embrace me unconditionally?

"Hey." Ryker came up to me and patted me on the shoulder. "Should you be out and about?"

"No concussion. Just a flesh wound." I moved down to a single picture of me. Above the frame was an owl. I pointed to the big blue-eyed baby. "Who's this?" I already knew, but did he?

"My baby brother."

"Silas?"

"No."

"Me?"

If it was possible for time to stand still, it did. Then, in slow motion, Ryker's normally stoic expression cracked. He reached out and pulled me into his arms. "Welcome home, little brother. It's so good to have you back."

Over his shoulder, I could see Ana in the doorway, her sweet smile making her tears look happy.

Ryker stepped back. "How did you know? Did Hannah tell you?"

Suddenly, my brain felt like it might explode. "Hannah knew?"

He nodded.

I wasn't sure how I felt about that. I'd been lied to all my life, and it was still happening. "When did you know?" I thought back to the day I met the brothers in my office. It was an odd meeting, but I didn't question it. Now I realized I should have been questioning everything.

Ryker pointed to an old leather chair, but I refused to sit. "We found out about you months ago. But we've been searching for you all our lives."

"And lying to me since we met." With my head aching and my heart shredded, I walked out.

Chapter 24

HANNAH

The owl clock's eyes shifted right and left, marking every minute I hadn't heard from Decker. He was supposed to call when he got home last night. Although I wanted to text him every ten minutes, I'd sent only one message asking him whether he was okay. That gash on his head was worrisome. And if I were honest with myself, I was also worried that his mother would talk him out of loving a common girl like me.

Only two couples occupied the diner. The snail's pace of the morning made not hearing from Decker worse. Nothing filled my time except thoughts of him.

The pot of coffee swung back and forth in my hand as I approached Mona and Marty's table. "Mornin', you two."

Marty looked up and grumbled. He may have been an early riser, but he wasn't a morning person.

"Marty." Mona elbowed him. "Hannah said hello." She had what could only be described as a teacher's admonishing voice. The kind that sent you to the timeout chair in the corner.

He lifted his eyes. "If you hadn't kept me up all night, I might be more pleasant."

She lifted her dark glasses, and a mischievous light sparkled in her clouded eyes. "Don't let him fool you, honey, he's insatiable in the sack. It was him who kept me up."

Rather than gag, I ignored her comment. "Cook made biscuits and gravy today."

"They stick to my dentures," Marty complained.

"Give the old geezer oatmeal. I'll take the special but add a scrambled egg. I need energy for round two."

"Damnit, Mona, the girl's going to think I'm a sex fiend."

Mona laughed. "At eighty-one, you should be telling everyone it still works." She looked at me. "It does, you know. It works fine."

"Good to know." My skin itched when I left the table. That sweater set and those tight white pin curls would never lead anyone to believe she had such a dirty mouth and an even dirtier mind.

To resist texting Decker was futile. While waiting for the old couple's meal, I rushed off another message.

Are you okay? Tell me the truth. I'm worried.

A reply didn't come back for minutes. And when it did, it took my breath away.

Save it, Hannah. Truth isn't your strong point.

The owl clock hooted eight times before I took my eyes off the screen of my phone. What the hell did that mean?

"Order up," the cook called.

I shoved my phone into my apron pocket and delivered the meals.

The bell above the door rang, and Silas and Ryker walked in. I approached with a full pot of coffee and several mugs in case the girls were joining them. They had that desperate-for-caffeine look about them.

"Have you heard from Decker?" Ryker plunked into the booth and dragged himself to the center of the bench.

"Yes. What the hell is going on?" I waited for Silas to take a seat, and I slid in next to him. "He called me a liar." I slapped my phone on the table. It lit up with his message about truth.

"I'm sorry, Hannah. This is my fault." Ryker picked up the phone and frowned. "He knows who he is. He came by last night, and I asked him if you told him."

"Shit, Ryker, I wanted to tell him, and you wouldn't let me," Hannah said.

Silas picked up the pot of coffee I'd brought and started to fill up the mugs. "That's my fault. I didn't want to disrupt his life if he was happy."

I threw myself against the booth back, hitting my head on the wooden frame. "Shit." I rubbed at the knot that was already forming. "He wasn't happy. He's been alone his whole life. His father is an asshole. His mother's a saint. His life is shit, and now it's shittier because he has no one." I flopped my head into my hands and cried.

"You told us he was happy," Ryker growled.

I swiped at the tears. "That was before I knew the truth."

"Spill it, Hannah. What's the truth?" Silas turned in my direction. Ryker scored me with sharp eyes. It was like an inquisition with both brothers staring me down.

I started at the beginning with the crash and worked my way to the hospital room where I'd left him, omitting the sexy bits. Those were reserved for me and me alone.

"You say this Tanner guy is his AA sponsor?" Ryker pulled out his phone and started tapping the screen. "The Dive is where he works?" His fingers skated across the smooth surface.

"No, Tanner owns The Dive," I said. "The place is special to Decker."

Ryker pulled out a ten and slapped it on the faded Formica table. "Let's go." He was out the door before I could say another word.

As soon as I got up, Silas filled up two cups of coffee and exited the booth. "I'll return these later."

I chased after him. "Silas, I love your brother. Make sure you tell him that."

He stopped with both hands full. "Hannah, I can tell him, but you need to show him. Let's make sure he knows he's loved."

"What's this about love?" Mona asked. "I couldn't help but hear."

I sank into the bench across from Marty and Mona and tapped a message on my phone.

Is withholding a truth the same as telling a lie? What if I was trying to stay loyal to friends, and it all got muddled? Don't judge me by one mistake. Give me a chance to make many more. We learn and grow from each other. I love you.

The old couple sat and listened to my problems like well-seasoned therapists, only cheaper.

"He'll come around," Marty said. "Men are stupid, but we can learn. Some of us take longer than others."

Mona reached across the table and set her hand near mine. I closed the gap so she could touch me. "You know that saying about how if you set someone free and they come back, they are yours forever?"

"Yes, I've heard it before." Was she trying to tell me to be patient?

"That's bullshit. You get your ass in your car and chase down that boy. Flick him on his stitches to get his attention and don't leave him until he's convinced you love him."

The whole visual frightened me, but it was Mona speaking, and no matter how quirky her delivery seemed, her message was always accurate.

"What if he doesn't love me anymore?"

"Oh, pish," she snorted. "If that boy doesn't love you, he doesn't deserve you."

"She's right," Marty added. "She's always right."

Mona smiled and nodded. "It's all in the training, dear." She patted Marty on the head like a good boy. "Sometimes a good man needs a little reminder of how lucky they are to have us. He's a Savage, so his reminder might need to be a bat to the head. Those boys are thick with stubbornness but worth the extra effort."

"Now, Mona," Marty piped in. "The girl's going to think you're being literal." Mona leaned over and whispered something into Marty's ear. He sat up straight. "She's right. Bring the bat." Marty blushed like a teenage boy with his first girly magazine. He turned toward the woman he obviously loved and said, "Can we use chocolate sauce this time?"

Mona smiled. "Of course, sweetheart, it's your favorite." She winked at me. "See, it's all in the training."

It took three hours and a busy lunch rush to get rid of the vision of Marty and Mona licking chocolate sauce off each other. When my replacement showed up, I rushed out the door and drove straight home.

Stacey was sitting on the couch with Nate. She was wearing a white T-shirt on which she'd written *Not Preggers* with a black marker. I didn't have the time or energy to analyze the situation any further, but I was glad that at least Nate was decent, had a job, and didn't have a record.

"Have you heard from Decker?" Nate asked as I flew past.

"No," I called from the hallway, "but he's going to hear from me."

Chapter 25

DECKER

"I'll have another." I lifted my mug toward the bartender, who happened to be Hannah's mom. She'd been working at The Dive for over a week. I'd come in at random times during the days hoping to avoid anyone I knew, but she was always here. At first, her hands shook like a leaf in a storm, but now she was solid. I remembered the DTs well. Days of praying to die if only to stop the shakes and shivers of detox.

"Hannah has been looking for you." Rachel was light on words, but each time she spoke it was always about her daughter. "I am only on step one, but I've read ahead. I think you should revisit the 'take personal inventory' step and admit that you were wrong. She didn't lie to you. She simply didn't tell you someone else's story. That's not a crime. In fact, most people would respect that."

I sipped at the root beer and set the mug down with a thunk. "I didn't come here for advice."

Tanner snuck up behind Rachel and wrapped his arms around her waist. They had obviously become close in the short amount of time they'd known each other. "You surely didn't come for the soda." Tanner nodded his head toward the corner booth.

Once we were both seated, he said, "Time to reconcile with yourself."

"Me? What the hell? There's certainly reconciling that needs to be done, but it's everyone else who owes me."

Tanner leaned forward, placing his elbows on the table. "You know the drill, Decker. Take care of you. Be honest with yourself. Be honest with others. Loving someone isn't a crime. Making the best decision, even if it's wrong, isn't necessarily nefarious."

I threaded my hands through my hair and tugged. The sting helped distract me from the pain I felt inside. "Everyone lied to me," I gritted out.

"Maybe, but was it done with malicious intent, or were they thinking of your feelings?"

Tanner had a point. It was the same message that ran through my head a hundred times a day. Was the secret kept to hurt me or help me? Each person had a different motive, and yet I'd poured all of them into the liar's container.

"I'm confused. I'm hurt. I'm lost." I glanced over at Hannah's mother and saw where Hannah got her good looks. God, I missed that girl. I was furious with everyone, including her, but I never stopped loving her.

"You have a right to be all those things, but don't push away the people who love you. They've all stopped in here looking for you. Ryker. Silas. Ana. Grace. Hannah. Even that old couple Marty and Mona. Reach out to them. They want to be a part of your life."

"I don't know where to begin."

"Start with your father. Don't let him die when you have words left unspoken. Be honest and be fair." Tanner rose from his seat and walked back to the bar.

I finished off my root beer and headed to the hospital.

THE ROOM WAS dark and foreboding when I entered. A quartet of monitors beeped and whistled and moaned. Dad lay frail and motionless in his bed.

For minutes I stared at him, wondering whether I'd ever truly known him. Mom was right. He was a perfectionist. He was a results-driven man who presented a failure-free image. Sadly, the world was about failure as much as it was about success.

Had I not drank myself to numbness early on, I may have faced a life like my father's—or, more specifically, a death like his. There were lessons in everything.

"Decker." Dad's parched voice broke through the cacophony.

I pulled up the chair where Mom often sat and took her place by his bed. "I'm here." I reached for his hand, which was completely unnatural, but Dad didn't pull away. In fact, he gripped me with his waning strength.

"I'm sorry." He began to cough and pointed to the cup next to his bed.

I held the straw to his lips and waited for him to sip. Water ran down his chin, and the look on his face was pure frustration. Dad never liked anyone to see his weakness. Hell, I'd never known he had any until recently.

"I'm sorry too."

"Your mother told you."

"Yes, and it all makes sense."

"I never hated you," he said. His voice thinned with each word.

"You never loved me either." I tried to let go of his hand, but he tightened his grip. It was as if I was his last lifeline to this world.

"Not true. I loved you the best way I knew how."

Tanner's talk about leaving words unspoken ran like a song on repeat. I could tell him all sorts of stuff he did to hurt me. All the ways I hated him. All the ways I wished he would have loved me. But what was the point? Not telling him wasn't a lie. It was a kindness. And Tanner's words about being fair won.

My stomach clenched like it had been doused in acid. Hannah and Ryker and Silas hadn't lied. They simply hadn't shared the truth because of the possibility that my life could have been better without it.

Maturity hadn't been my strongest attribute this week. I'd acted selfishly and childishly out of hurt. I'd not let my father die with angry words as the last ones he heard.

"Do you remember my first sale? You dressed me in a suit and tie like I was your partner." We were a matching pair. I was his mini-me.

His yellow eyes brightened. "You were my partner."

"That was the best day ever. I sold a house. We went to Scoops for ice cream, and you let me sit in your chair the entire day at your office."

"You remembered."

"That was a good day. What about when I superglued your desk drawers shut?"

"Not such a good day. I had a board meeting, and my notes were in there."

"I wanted you to go to lunch with me."

"You got your wish." His head fell forward but flopped back against the pillow. After several tries to sit up, he gave up.

"If I remember correctly, you made me pay everyone an hour's pay for their wasted time." I laughed.

"Time is money," we both said at the same time.

"About that, Decker. If I had to do it all over again ..." He stalled. "I'd spend more time doing kid things with you. We should have played ball and gone to the park to fly kites."

I closed my eyes and pictured moments like that. It seemed like an unbelievable dream. That's not who Rip Riley and I were. I opened my eyes. Really opened my eyes for the first time. "We parsed numbers and sold properties. It's all the same. You lose some, you win some." That's who we were. We were Riley and son. He wasn't all hugs and praise, but he was my father.

"Do you hate the family business?"

This was one time I didn't want to lie. "Yes, but I'll do it because it's your legacy."

Dad struggled to lean forward. He let go of my hand and reached for the button for the bed. He raised himself to a seated position. "And what will yours be? The man who hated himself more than he hated real estate? I don't want that for you."

It was the first time I'd heard Dad consider my wants, or maybe it was the first time I'd listened. "What do you want from me?"

He grasped my hand again. "I want you to be happy, Decker. In the end, you can't take any of it with you. I thought I'd die happy knowing you'd be taking the helm of what I created, but that's my accomplishment, and when I'm gone, it no longer matters. What do you want to accomplish? When you're lying on your deathbed, what will you see as your greatest achievement?"

"I met a woman that I want to make a part of my life. I want to revitalize communities that have suffered a blow like Fury."

"I never paid much attention to your past. Once you were ours, the past never mattered." He took a few labored breaths. "I always thought that if I couldn't have my DNA in you, then I'd put my work ethic and passion in you."

That was where I'd fallen short in my father's eyes. "I'm sorry I was a disappointment."

"You weren't, Decker. I was simply shortsighted. You have the business; make it what you want. Open a division that does exactly what you want it to do. Fall in love, make babies, play softball, fly kites."

I didn't dare let the tear that gathered in my eye fall. There was no way I'd let Rip Riley know that I was weak. I was more like him than he'd ever know.

"A party without me." Mom walked in looking like she'd left the spa, which was funny because she wasn't a spa kind of girl. However, she was a Riley, and we always pulled our shoulders back and pressed forward.

"Yep, Dad and I were getting ready to get out of here and fly a kite." I smiled at my father, who had drifted off to sleep.

"I'm game. How about a picnic and afterward, we can watch the sun set?" Mom said.

The rest of the afternoon was spent talking about our lives as a family with dad moving in and out of consciousness. And when the sun set for the day, so it set on my father's life. He took his last breath with me holding his hand. He may not have brought me into this world, but I held him while he left it.

Chapter 26

HANNAH

I f not for Tanner and my mother, no one would have known about Decker's father's passing. Although not invited, we showed up en masse at the funeral. It was a large affair with hundreds of people in attendance. I sat in the back row of the church with Ryker and Ana, Silas and Grace, Tanner and Mom, and Stacey and Nate. Marty and Mona stayed behind in Fury to babysit.

When the service was over, we walked past the front pew where Decker sat with his mom. His eyes lit up when he saw us. That sparkle gave me hope.

He stood when I neared. "You look beautiful." There was more in his eyes than those three words.

"Thank you." I looked down at my charcoal gray dress. It was the closest thing to black I could come up with. I never understood the wearing of black at a funeral. In my opinion, a life should be celebrated, not mourned, and celebration came in full color—but I respected the tradition.

"We need to talk, but this isn't the time. Can I call you?"

I swore my jaw hit the floor. "I've been waiting for your call for days." I tried not to let my hurt show, but it was impossible. Love hurt.

"I know. I have a lot to say, but not here."

The line was backing up, so I moved forward to give my condolences to his mother.

"Hannah, thanks for coming." Though her eyes were rimmed with red, she looked so put together and composed.

"I wanted to be here."

As I moved to the side, I heard Decker introduce Ryker and Silas. "Mom, you met them once before, but these are my brothers." Could anything have sounded more perfect? Sadly, yes, but as Decker said, our words would come later. This wasn't the time.

We exited the church to find at least a dozen kites in the air. In big letters across the bright fabric were the words *family, love, patience, kindness, hope,* and others I couldn't make out because they were so high in the sky, skimming the heavens.

I waited all day and night for a call that didn't come and trudged into work the next day ready to take my frustration out on unsuspecting diners. They wouldn't know that the French toast in their lap helped ease my heartache, or the spilled soda cooled my temper. It was way better than sitting in my car and crying.

Three cleanups into my morning, the bell above the door rang. A large bouquet with a set of legs walked into the diner, and my heart stalled. A head peeked around the blooms. "Delivery for Hannah Banning."

"That's me!" I squealed. I signed for the flowers and slapped some dollar bills into the guy's hand.

I searched through the stems to find the card. Tucked in between two red roses, I pulled it free and ran my fingertips over my name on the outside of the tiny envelope.

I said a prayer and pulled the card from inside.

You and me
Dinner
Tonight
Six o'clock
Boulder Dushanbe Teahouse
I'll send a car to pick you up at home.
See you there, Hannah
Love,

Decker (The man begging you to love him again.)

JOHN PICKED me up in the black town car at precisely five o'clock. My heart raced all the way to Boulder. Dressed in the pink sundress Decker had bought for me in Vail, I felt ready to face whatever this was. In truth, I knew it couldn't be bad given the flowers and the way he signed the card like he was asking me to love him. How could I not? I'd known I was in trouble the minute he walked into the diner, and once he'd mopped the floor, I was a goner.

As a backup, I brought a bat. Mona might have been teasing, but I wasn't beyond beating him upside the head if he led me on again.

The car pulled to a stop in front of the walkway, and John opened my door. I reached in for the bat that I'd borrowed from Ana. If she thought it odd, she said nothing.

"You won't need that." John pried my fingers from the handle. "If he screws this up, I'll beat him for you myself."

I didn't know John well, but I liked him. He was a loyal sort—that kind of man you wanted by your side through thick and thin.

"I'll hold you to that." My heels clicked along the cement. Fully bloomed roses scented the air. A nearby stream bubbled in the distance. The tranquil setting put confidence in my step, if not my heart, as I entered the restaurant. If this wasn't a moment that called for alcohol, I couldn't name one that did. Since Mom was sobering up, I couldn't even grab some liquid courage before I left the house.

I looked around for Decker, but he was nowhere in sight. Figured. And of course, it was my luck that the same girl manned the hostess stand.

I did an internal eye roll before pasting on my screw-you smile. If she said one cross word to me, I was running for the bat.

When she looked up, her eyes widened, and her lips formed a smile, albeit a small one. "Hello, Hannah."

Her use of my name almost knocked me off my heels. "Hello," I said with caution.

The girl looked flustered. "I have to get this right."

She pulled a note from under the stack of menus. "Mr. Riley said that he would be honored if you would join him on the patio." She looked up and smiled as if she'd recited the Constitution by heart. "He says—" She cleared her throat. "—that he's a stupid idiot and he loves you." For dramatic effect, she tapped her chest right about where her hollow heart must have resided. "He also says that if you'll take a chance on a future with him, he's waiting in the rose garden."

I turned around and ran outside. From behind me, I could hear the girl mutter, "So I guess that's a yes."

There was outdoor dining on the left and right. One area was empty, one was full. At the edge of the vacant patio stood Decker dressed in black slacks and a gray Henley. In his arms was another bunch of flowers.

I raced to him. "Are those for me?"

"Maybe."

I plucked a rose from the top of the bouquet and brought it to my nose. "Maybe?"

He smiled, and my rib cage ached with the swelling of my heart.

"It's a package deal. If you take the flowers, you get me."

The sweet fragrance of the petals mixed with his cologne to create the perfect heady scent. It raced through my veins and tugged at my heart. God, I'd missed him. I'd never experienced addiction, but if it felt like this, I knew I'd never beat it.

Playing hard to get, I walked past him into the patio that he'd obviously reserved for us. A single table sat next to the bubbling brook, and at least ten teapots lined nearby serving trays. All the tea we never tasted on our last failed trip to Dushanbe.

He trailed behind me. He was like a live wire arcing off me. We sizzled together and fizzled apart. I knew this for certain. I'd tried to talk myself out of loving him, but I couldn't. I was angry, but I'd never woken up one day without wanting to see Decker again or feel his touch. That alone granted him leeway.

"A package deal, huh?" I turned around to face him. "I don't know. It's a lot to deal with. I mean…" I leaned into his body and whispered against his lips, "What am I supposed to do with all these flowers?"

He tossed the blooms to the ground and pulled me into his arms. "Forget the flowers."

I looked into his blue eyes. So sorry. So sexy. So sincere. "How about you do me instead?" I pressed my lips to his and took every bit of love he offered.

When we broke for air, Decker raised his hand to the waiter who stood nearby.

"Check, please."

Chapter 27

DECKER-ONE YEAR LATER

W e took up an entire row at Hannah's graduation. I sat on the end of the aisle so I could get a good picture when she walked across the stage. My girl had finished her degree, and she was heading back for her master's right away because she'd found her passion in helping others. My heart was full to bursting with pride, both that she'd come so far, and that I could call her mine.

Little did she know that I was and would continue to be her most successful patient.

Mom sat beside me. Next to her was Rachel. The two moms, despite their dissimilarities, had become friends. In the end, none of us were all that different. The only thing that separated us was compassion, and once you opened your heart, there was no limit to the amount of joy people could bring to your life.

Flapping above me was a kite to honor my father. He had wanted to see me happy, and so I brought this reminder with me wherever I could. It soared above me, always reminding me to look up and to appreciate the moments we had because all too soon they were gone, and you couldn't get them back.

I looked down the row of seats to my brothers, who sat with their wives and children. They had run through hell and lived. We had all survived and had come out better people for it.

Silas held Blue while Grace held an empty bucket in case she got sick. Morning sickness had plagued her for the past few months. In the fall I'd be an uncle again.

Ryker sat tall and proud. He was the backbone of our family, and Ana was where he got his strength. Little Wren slept peacefully in his mother's arms. Nate had his arm around Stacey. They were headed to college together this fall with a lifetime supply of condoms courtesy of Hannah. Marty and Mona sat at the other end. Marty nodded off to sleep here and there, but you couldn't blame the man; by all accounts, he was the stud all of us aspired to be. Mona was all spit and vinegar on the outside, but she was sweetness and light inside. And she still made the best lemonade and hot chocolate in town.

Pomp and Circumstance played. My skin prickled with excitement. This was the first day of the rest of our lives. I'd sold the flat in Golden and moved everything to Fury. Hannah and I lived above the garage in the house where my life had begun.

And if I was lucky, I'd be able to bring joy and happiness back into its walls with my own children someday.

"Hannah Banning." Her name echoed through the auditorium, and I jumped from my seat. Our group hooted and howled until she blushed with embarrassment. She stood at the edge of the stage and thrust her diploma high into the air.

At the top of her lungs, she yelled, "This is for my family, the ones I was born to, and the ones I chose." Her eyes scanned the row and stopped at me. "I love you, Owl."

It turned out I had my own bird name, and why shouldn't I? I was a Savage by birth. I lived in a nest, and I was raised under the wings of people who loved me.

I was there at the end of the stairs waiting for her. She jumped into my arms, and I twirled her until we were both dizzy.

"Oh. My. God." She kissed me hard. "Could this day get any better?"

"Maybe," I said before I set her down and dropped to my knees.

"Maybe?"

"It would get a lot better if you married me. If you promised to be mine for life. If someday we could hatch our own little eggs." I held out the ring I'd chosen for her. Not too big. Not too small. Perfect for the perfect woman.

She stared at the box for a moment too long, and I worried that she'd say no. But Hannah did what Hannah did best. She tapped her invisible bat against my head.

"I don't know. It's a lot to deal with. I mean …" She let me slip the ring on her finger. "What am I supposed to do with you?"

I pressed my lips to hers and whispered. "Love me."

She leaned back and said, "I already do."

Chapter 28

HANNAH - FIVE YEARS LATER

"Grab the present," I said as I picked up the cake and headed for the door. Today was a big day. It was Mona's birthday.

"Got it," Decker said. He'd raced inside the house after an early morning ride with his brothers. He lifted our two-year-old son, Ripley, onto his hip and reached for the gift. He never let me carry anything now that I was pregnant again.

We climbed into the Range Rover and drove under a sign that read *Abundance: A Boys of Fury Development*. Decker had kept Ripley Realty but had changed its focus from profit to prosperity for all. He was still rich as sin because once the coffers got as full as his did, it was hard to spend it down, but we tried. Our goal was to be broke when we died. The best gift we could leave our kids was memories of hours well spent.

We drove through the neighborhood once filled with empty, sad, little houses; today, it was bursting at the seams with families and small children. The community park was awash in streamers, balloons, and people waiting for the town's favorite octogenarian to show up for her birthday party.

If I knew Mona, she was getting what she called a little bump and tickle before she left the house. Her motto was *live until you die*, and that was as good as any motto I knew.

Peggy rushed over to the car to kiss her favorite little man. Not Decker. Ripley. Although our son didn't share DNA with his paternal grandparents, I swore he favored Decker's father with his keen eye and his love for the abacus Peggy had bought him for Christmas.

Wren and Blue played in the sandbox while their little sisters toddled about. Grace and Silas had had a girl four years ago and named her Robin, while Ana and Ryker named their daughter Raven. Ripley hadn't come out of the naming game unscathed, either: His full name was Ripley Kite Savage Riley. It seemed fitting that a kite was a symbol of Decker's love for his father and also a bird of prey.

Nate carried a pot of chili while Stacey waddled behind him. She was days away from delivering their first child. With the size of her, everyone thought it was two, but they promised it was one chubby little boy they would name Cody.

Even Tanner and Rachel had added to their family by way of a yellow Lab named Beau.

"Here they come!" yelled Ana.

Marty thunked his walker across the grass while Mona did her best to not leave him behind. When they got close enough, everyone laughed. Marty was wearing more of Mona's orange lipstick than she was, and her shirt was on backward. But that was standard for the odd, older couple.

They were quirky, but they were real, and we liked real. They taught everyone what life was about, and it had nothing to do with money. It was as simple as sharing wisdom over a glass of lemonade or your problems over a cup of hot chocolate. Not the fake kind you get in packets, but the real stuff you find in a green and yellow owl mug.

Mona's Lemonade

There's nothing better than a wicker chair, a porch, and a cup of lemonade on a hot summer day. I would never use powder, so here's my tried-and-true recipe. It's practically a family heirloom, so keep it safe.

Ingredients

• 10 wax-free lemons, preferably organic because who needs all that wax in their bodies? If I want to preserve myself, I'll use whiskey.

• 2 cups sugar. I like the cane, but light brown sugar will do just fine.

• 1 ½ cups cold water

Directions

Remove the zest but not the white squishy part from the lemons using a vegetable peeler or a zester. Juice the lemons. You need 1 1/2 cups juice. Place all the zest and juice in a saucepan, add the sugar and water, and heat slowly over medium heat, stirring constantly, until the sugar has dissolved. The liquid should approach boiling but should not actually boil.

Remove from the heat. Strain the mixture and discard the lemon zest and any seeds. You should have about 4 cups of sweet lemony goodness. Let it cool because it's lemonade, not hot tea. Although it's good to add to tea too.

Pour the syrup into a clean bottle and let it cool. I love to use Mason jars. Syrup will last up to two weeks (or a day and a half during summer in Fury).

For each serving, stir 1 part syrup with 3 parts water. Add ice. Sit back and watch the pink flamingos on your lawn. In my neighborhood, they seem to reproduce. I think there's something magic in the lemonade.

Mona's Hot Chocolate

Hot chocolate is a winter staple in my kitchen, but I'd never settle for the powdered brands. It's all or nothing with this old girl.

Ingredients

• 1 milk chocolate or dark chocolate candy bar, chopped, or use those little mini-chips because they melt faster. At my age, I want to enjoy my hot cocoa before I die.

• 2/3 cup milk, or more to taste. Or be decadent and use half and half. It may send you into a cardiac arrest, but death by chocolate doesn't sound so bad.

• 1 pinch ground cinnamon (optional)

• A shot of Bailey's if you dare. I sneak it into Marty's cup when I want some sexy time.

Directions

Place chocolate pieces in a saucepan over medium-low heat; add milk and whisk constantly until chocolate is melted and blended. Stir in optional ingredients. (Yes, that means the Bailey's.) Remove from heat; add more milk if desired or more Bailey's. Serve in an owl mug.

Other Books by Kelly Collins

The Boys of Fury Series

Redeeming Ryker

Saving Silas

Delivering Decker

The Boys of Fury Boxset

Wilde Love Series

Betting On Him

Betting On Her

Betting On Us

A Wilde Love Collection

Get a free book.

Go to www.authorkellycollins.com

About the Author

International bestselling author of more than thirty novels, Kelly Collins writes with the intention of keeping love alive. Always a romantic, she blends real-life events with her vivid imagination to create characters and stories that lovers of contemporary romance, new adult, and romantic suspense will return to again and again.

For More Information
www.authorkellycollins.com
kelly@authorkellycollins.com

Acknowledgments

What a glorious experience this series was to write. Here I thought I'd write about a few brothers who had lost their way, and in the end I had an entire town that knew the value of love and helped them find their way back.

Mona seemed to be a fan favorite and she was modeled after an old neighbor I had by the name of Dorothy who was nearly blind. She told me she came with my lease when I moved into the house next-door to hers.

I learned a lot from Dorothy, but mostly I laughed at her antics. Sadly she passed away several years ago and with her a little bit of sunshine in this world was dimmed.

Books never get written without the love and support of a village. My village is my family and friends and fans who never cease to surprise me with their unending love and support. Thanks for everything you do to make the hours of writing worthwhile. With love,

Kel

Printed in Great Britain
by Amazon

38945046R00106